CW00517079

A ROGUE IN THE MAKING

Forever Yours Series

STACY REID

Edited by AuthorsDesigns
Cover design and formatting by AuthorsDesigns

Dusean, always and forever.

FREE OFFER

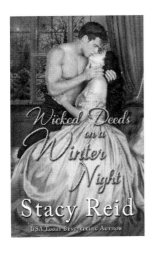

To claim your FREE copy of Wicked Deeds on a Winter Night, a delightful and sensual romp to indulge in your reading addiction, please click here.

Once you've signed up, you'll be among the first to hear about my new releases, read excerpts you won't find anywhere else, and patriciate in subscriber's only giveaways and contest. I send out on dits once a month and on super special occasion I might send twice, and please know you can unsubscribe whenever we no longer zing.

Happy reading!

Stacy Reid

"Wicked in His Arms—Once again Stacy Reid has left me spellbound by her beautifully spun story of romance between two wildly different people."—*Meghan L., LadywithaQuill.com*

"Wicked in His Arms—I truly adored this story and while it's very hard to quantify, this book has the hallmarks of the great historical romance novels I have read!"—*KiltsandSwords.com*

"One for the ladies...**Sins of a Duke** is nothing short of a romance lover's blessing!"—*WTF Are You Reading*

"THE ROYAL CONQUEST is raw, gritty and powerful, and yet, quite unexpectedly, it is also charming and endearing."—*The Romance Reviews*

OTHER BOOKS BY STACY

Series Boxsets

Forever Yours Series Bundle (Book 1-3)

Forever Yours Series Bundle (Book 4-6)

Forever Yours Series Bundle (Book 7-9)

The Amagarians: Book 1-3

The Kincaids series bundle (Books 1-3)

Sinful Wallflowers series

My Darling Duke

Her Wicked Marquess

Forever Yours series

The Marquess and I

The Duke and I

The Viscount and I

Misadventures with the Duke

When the Earl was Wicked

A Prince of my Own

Sophia and the Duke

The Sins of Viscount Worsley

For the Love of the Earl

Mischief and Mistletoe

A Rogue in the Making

My One and Only Earl

The Kincaids

Taming Elijah

Tempting Bethany

Lawless: Noah Kincaid

Moonlight Magic: Jenny Kincaid

Rebellious Desires series

Duchess by Day, Mistress by Night

The Earl in my Bed

Wedded by Scandal Series

Accidentally Compromising the Duke

Wicked in His Arms

How to Marry a Marquess

When the Earl Met His Match

Scandalous House of Calydon Series

The Duke's Shotgun Wedding

The Irresistible Miss Peppiwell

Sins of a Duke

The Royal Conquest

The Amagarians

Eternal Darkness

Eternal Flames

Eternal Damnation

Eternal Phoenyx

Eternal Promise

Single Titles

Letters to Emily

Wicked Deeds on a Winter Night

The Scandalous Diary of Lily Layton

CHAPTER 1

K nock. *Knock. Knock.*
The harsh rap of her knuckles on the large oak door reverberated up Miss Juliana Pryce's arm, but she stalwartly pressed onward. *Knock. Knock. Knock.* She tried the doorbell a few times to no avail, and desperation lent her the strength to slam her fist against the door. The chill of the early winter wind bit at her bones and the sun was a mere decoration in the gray overcast sky, for it afforded no heat to her body. This fall promised to be dreary and bitingly cold. Perhaps it might even snow this December.

The door opened, and a sharp breath of relief left her. "I'm Miss Juliana Pryce, and I am here to call upon Lord Spencer Prendergast. Please announce me immediately. It is about to rain."

The butler looked down his nose at her, and Juliana winced, perfectly capable of imagining her own bedraggled appearance. She'd jumped from a moving carriage and then had hidden in the bushes for quite a long time. Her trek to London had been long, frightening, and had involved traveling for some time in a hay cart and other vehicles, before striding up the cobbled streets of Mayfair.

"Lord Prendergast is not at home to callers," the butler said with a small wrinkle of his nose.

"My good man, you'll inform him that Miss Juliana Pryce, sister to Mr. Robert Pryce, requests an audience most urgently. They are friends, and I must prevail upon him regarding a request from my brother. Forgive my rudeness, but I will not leave until I have seen the earl. Even if I have to stand here and make an exhibition of myself for hours which I assure you will cause terrible speculation."

An empty threat, but given her air of desperation and dishevelment, the man might believe her. And he did, for he eased the door open and allowed her inside.

"May I take your coat and bonnet?"

With trembling fingers, she untied the strings to her bonnet and coat, handing them over to the waiting butler. He led her down the long hallway and into a small room, which seemed to be a private parlor. Once there, she made her way to the fire, grateful for the crackling flames. The room appeared decorated in the late Baroque style, or Rococo with considerable ornamentation, but in anachronistic reds and purples.

The color scheme was rather oppressive, especially against the ornamentation of gilded moldings and cluttered surfaces. An ormolu clock of great size, and fantastical design, sat on the over mantel. It was embellished with nymphs, putti, and forest creatures, which Juliana thought were particularly unattractive.

The plethora of trinkets and baubles appeared to have been chosen for their cost, rather than in any aesthetic style or overall plan. The room shrieked, 'I am wealthy and do not have a jot of taste.' Juliana noticed overstuffed upholstery and tasseled cushions in a variety of complicated patterns. She did not sit in any of them, feeling somewhat overpowered by the décor and fearing it would suck her into the overwhelming chintz and tapestries. Juliana didn't have to wait long for the door to open and Lord Prendergast to enter.

Juliana observed a gentleman in his mid-thirties with a high complexion and excessive dark eyebrows that seemed to take over his face. They were in contrast to his brutally shorn mousy hair and somewhat sparse mustache. His waistline was already showing a tendency to corpulence, and she suspected it would not be long before he gained at least an extra chin.

"Miss Pryce!" he said, considerably surprised. "Are you aware of the hour?"

"I think it might be as early as ten, my lord. I interrupted you breaking your fast. I apologize."

He hesitated, his gaze sweeping the room. "You are without a chaperon."

A shaky laugh slipped from her. "I am afraid I am, but it could not be helped. And at my advanced age of four and twenty, I believe I am allowed some moderation from propriety."

His gaze raked over her, coolly appraising. "I can see that you've had some difficulties traveling here. Please, tell me what has driven you to my doorstep at this hour."

"My brother... Mr. Robert Pryce... before he left for

America, he named you as a gentleman I could visit should I ever need help."

"Yes, Robert and I are acquaintances," he murmured, sitting on a wing-back chair near the fireplace.

She noted the distinction in his words and that he did not claim friendship. Her brother was very wealthy. Many fine people of society clamored to be his 'friend,' even if they were tentative about inviting him to their elevated circles. A shiver of foreboding went through her, and she shrugged it away. Given her morning so far, it was easy to be suspicious about everything.

"Would you like me to take that?"

It was then Juliana realized she still held the umbrella, which she had stolen from the carriage more to use as a weapon than protection from the rain, clutched in her grip.

The butler hadn't even asked her for it. Perhaps she was just too unsettled from escaping a most nefarious plot to see her married off for her inheritance.

"No, that is fine, I'll hold on to it for now." Her chin rose. "I was dragged from my home a few hours ago with the express purpose of being forced into a marriage with Mr. Matthew Chevers."

Surprise flared in the earl's eyes. "Your brother?"

"My stepfather's son," she said. "I assure you, Mr. Chevers is not my brother."

"Good God, and you say he tried to force you to marry him?"

"Yes, and he had the permission of Viscount Bramley." The man who had married her mother three years ago, and her stepfather.

"His son, the despicable bounder, tried to enact his

plans last night. I cannot return home, for surely they will only try again."

Matthew had recently bestowed a flattering amount of attention upon Juliana, and it had been puzzling, for he had barely tolerated her presence when they'd first met. And over the years, while he had been cordial, he hadn't been over friendly. A bitter flavor of distaste coated her tongue. His attentions had not been genuine, and thankfully she hadn't been charmed, merely suspicious. Seeing her lack of gratitude that Matthew would consider marrying, "a lady firmly on the shelf," as his father had snidely put it. They had decided on a more diabolical plan.

If her dear papa had not raised her to be independent and to take action for herself, she would have been married to the bounder already. "My mother is in Bath recovering from a malady, so I cannot burden her."

Not that her mother had the power to influence the viscount's decision, who oddly doted on his lady, despite his plot to try to control Juliana's life and her inheritance. Her mother even seemed to love the man. Juliana could not see the point of burdening her ailing mother with her husband's deceit. Not when it would hurt her heart. Worse, Juliana feared her mother might even agree with the viscount. For she thought Juliana's dream to be in control of her own money and to continue some of her father's work nonsensical.

"Robert told me whatever I need you might assist me with."

An unknown emotion flicked over the earl's face. "And how do you need my help?"

Juliana wondered exactly what the earl was thinking,

but suspected it involved irritation at having to deal with her problems. She did not believe the earl was especially receptive to her plight, for she felt no touch of fellow feeling in the man.

"I got a recent letter from Robert to say he is returning to London and he should be here before the end of December. It is tempting to book the fastest ship to New York, but that would still take six weeks to arrive, and Robert and I might miss each other. England has only been my home these past four years. I am pragmatic enough to know I cannot escape my stepfather's plans with the few resources I own at present. So, I must position myself in a place where they cannot reach me until my brother returns home."

"And this is where I come in," he said, his gaze probing and even a bit discomfiting.

That had been her desperate reasoning when the kind farmer taking his produce to market had picked her up. "Yes. My father's will specified that if I were not married by five and twenty, it meant I know my mind. So my inheritance will be handed over to me—half on my twenty-fifth birthday and the last half on my thirtieth birthday. I gather my stepfather means to force me by any means necessary to marry his son before my birthdate in two months' time, and I mean to escape their nefarious plotting by any means necessary. Obviously, as I will access my fortune then, any financial expenses involved would be promptly repaid."

The earl stared at her for a long time before saying, "I see your plight, Miss Pryce. Please stay here, I will be back shortly."

To her dismay, he rose and quickly left the room. Juliana stood and started to pace. A young maid entered with a tea trolley and sandwiches. Her stomach rumbled alarmingly, and despite her unease and agitated nerves, she drank two cups of tea and ate several delicate sandwiches. Her hunger satisfied, she stood and resumed her pacing by the windows. Once she sat still, the terror and fury of the last several hours swamped her senses, and her hands shook. The bounders! How had they dared act in such a despicable fashion!

The door to the small drawing-room opened, and the earl entered.

"Forgive my delay," he said with a smile. "I had to send off an urgent missive. Please, sit, Miss Pryce. Have you had some tea?"

Releasing a pent-up breath, she slowly sat. "I've had two cups, my lord."

"You still look frightfully pale," he murmured sympathetically.

"I was recently trussed up in a carriage and bound for God knows where," she said drily. "I dare say it might take a few days for me to recover my composure."

Beneath his slashing ebony brows, the earl's blue eyes narrowed at her in contemplation. "Isn't the best thing to simply marry, Miss Pryce?"

Juliana's heart jolted. "Why is that the best solution, my lord?"

"You need a man's good sense to manage such wealth. There is a rumor it is five hundred thousand pounds, a large country house in Hertfordshire, and substantial shares in your brother's shipping company."

The intimate details of her inheritance were much discussed in the *ton*, but she hadn't thought he would so baldly discuss money. Her limited experience with the marriage mart revealed Juliana's dowry was her chief attraction for any suitor. It did not endear her heart to any gentleman. "I value my independence, and I am far more sensible with finances than most gentlemen of society who find themselves desperate to marry heiresses because they squandered their opportunities and the trust that was invested in them."

"I see." His smile did not reach his eyes. "Have you considered that Lord Bramley is protecting your best interest? Surely you cannot believe your stepfather is a fortune hunter, and his son... Matthew... we know each other, and I tell you he is a good sport and you would make him an excellent wife."

"He would not make me an excellent husband."

"Come now, Miss Pryce," the earl chided. "You cannot know—"

"I know," she retorted, swallowing an unpleasant lump in her throat.

Juliana offered him a small smile that was exceedingly difficult to drum up, considering the anxiety beating inside her chest. "If I am to ever marry, it will be for one reason only. That I love the man I would spend the rest of my life with. Surely you agree, my lord, that it is not a flimsy undertaking to share your heart and life with another. I would only want such an attachment with a gentleman I held in esteem. Not one who would contrive to steal my choices and my inheritance that my father worked extremely hard to leave to his children. Now was my brother wrong to urge me to your doorsteps, my lord?"

"Of course not." Yet he oozed insincerity.

Juliana felt a measure of panic. She'd dearly hoped Lord Prendergast would help her. If not, she would turn to the second name her brother had left with her, Lord Rawlings. Another earl, and possibly another gentleman who would think she should accept her fate because she was merely a woman.

His butler entered after a brief knock, and a silent message passed between them. Juliana frowned when the earl excused himself once more. She hurriedly stood, went over to the door, and eased it open. Shock blasted through her in icy waves. Lord Prendergast was greeting her stepfather in the hallway and exchanging words with him. They laughed together, and she could see the easy bonhomie between the earl and the jovial looking gray-haired Viscount Bramley.

Good heavens. The missive the earl had sent earlier had been to her stepfather. Juliana closed the door, twisting the key in the lock with a *snick*, then whirled around looking for an avenue of escape.

The earl had either not believed her story, or he thought her plight was not his problem. Juliana could not allow her stepfather to force her to leave with him. She would prefer to haul herself on the ground and start a scandal. But then he might be as underhanded as he had been yesterday. After taking dinner in her room on a tray, she had woken in a carriage, headed for God's know where with Matthew inside.

She tamped down a burgeoning sense of panic. Juliana

needed the time to think and craft a plan. God, her coat and bonnet had to be left behind. She rushed toward the large sash windows, pushed the lacy drapes to one side, then shoved the lower window open. She swung a leg up over the ledge and clambered through it into the pelting rain. It was challenging with her wide skirts and petticoats. Still, she managed to escape without tearing her bedraggled gown. She did not bother to close the window behind her or look back. Within minutes she was soaked and trembling. Juliana quickly ran along the side of the townhouse and through a small wrought-iron gate into the streets. A speeding carriage lumbered by and splashed puddles of water onto her dress. She opened the large black umbrella, violently shaking under the chill of the rain.

Recalling that the second gentleman Robert had directed her to trust lived close by, she walked as fast as she could, head bent low to avoid the stinging rain against her face. It had been her good fortune Lord Prendergast had not withdrawn to the country. Juliana hoped she would have similar luck with the Earl of Rawlings. Several minutes passed before she arrived in Berkeley Square, looking like a drowned cat. The umbrella provided little protection against the sleeting rain and winds. Marching up to the front door, she knocked several times and waited.

The door opened, and the butler loomed a displeasing look on his face.

"I'm Miss Juliana Pryce and—"

"Go around to the servant's entrance," he clipped, then closed the door in her face.

Juliana spluttered. "How abominably rude!"

Clearly, this man indicated a master with a similar temperament. Or Lord Rawlings did not have his staff in hand. Still, she obeyed, desperate to escape the chilling downpour. Reaching the servant's entrance, she knocked and was allowed to enter a large kitchen that immediately enveloped her in warmth.

"You are soaked through, aren't you?" A plump-faced woman asked, dusting off her apron. "'Tis a sorry sight you are, and too late."

"Too late?" Juliana asked, standing still in the puddle she made on the stone floor. It was a relief to see a friendly face.

"Aren't you here for the housekeeper's position? It was filled over two hours ago. The only vacancy is for milord's valet, and it needs to be filled right away since he must depart tomorrow."

"Oh, I am not here for a job," she hurriedly assured the amiable woman who seemed to be the cook. "I wish an audience with the earl. It is most urgent!"

"You and everybody," the cook muttered, walking over to a large wooden board, and started to chop shallots with impressive speed.

"I beg your pardon?"

"You will just have to stand in line like everybody else and wait till milord is available. He is off somewhere, and it might take weeks for him to surface."

Her heart sank. "He is not here?"

"He's here all right, but he's not *here* if you know what I mean."

Juliana most certainly did not, and she stared at the woman, decidedly baffled. "I do not understand."

"Milord's nose is buried in one of his books, and he'll not be home to anyone until he's come out of the book. It is the way of things with milord."

"This is an emergency," Juliana said, swiping at the rivulet on her forehead.

"Unless the house is burning down, you must make an appointment like everyone else," the cook said. "The only thing milord needs is a valet, for he intends to set off for his country estate tomorrow. Mr. Hanson is none too pleased with how topsy-turvy everything is."

"Mr. Hanson?" she asked, wiping the water from her cheek.

"The butler. He's not happy that the master is to travel down without a manservant."

"The earl is leaving?"

The cook frowned. "'Tis normal for his lordship to withdraw once all his duties in the House of Lords are over."

"And where is the earl going?"

The cook frowned at her. "To his country seat in Sussex."

The earl was retiring to his country estate tomorrow and would likely be there for the rest of the year. Disappointment lodged heavily against her heart. A few minutes later, Juliana was standing outside. The bleakness of the sky was a perfect reflection of her mood. Her throat burned, and her eyes ached intolerably. It was very tempting to give in to all the raw, chaotic feelings and cry. "I will not allow them to steal my choices," she whispered fiercely. "But what am I to do?"

Her mother had allowed the viscount to take over

administering Juliana's monthly allowance, and he had withheld it for the last three months. Her mother acted frail and flustered when Juliana and the viscount had argued. Her stepfather had accused her of being far too independent with her spending, and her mother had apologized on her daughter's behalf.

Juliana blew out a sharp breath. How it infuriated her that someone she had given her trust to have placed her in this awful predicament. Only a few months ago, she'd thought her mother's new husband was someone to hold in high esteem and had given him her respect. How short-sighted that had been. He had appeared such a nice man who treated her mother so well. The idea that her fortune would not remain in his family had been too big a temptation for him to resist. At first, his son had been fairly charming. He had done his best to court her, but the more she had spent time with Matthew Chevers, the more she found she disliked him.

With a sigh, Juliana glanced back at the townhouse. She had heard the rumors that labeled the young earl an eccentric, albeit a brilliant one. He'd completed his University studies at seventeen, a feat that was very unusual in English society. Her brother had called him a good friend and seemed to ardently admire the earl.

Perhaps he, too, would have alerted her stepfather. Juliana's presence might well have been a nuisance, a distraction from his precious books. "What do I do?" she whispered, her throat aching.

Juliana walked away, with no direction in mind. She had little money, and the people known to her in Town were more acquaintances than genuine friends. "What I need is to hide in plain sight."

Preferably away from London and Derbyshire.

Sussex, maybe.

Juliana froze, her thoughts furiously churning. Could she infiltrate the Earl of Rawlings's household and plead her case? Perhaps assess his character before she told him of her plight. The earl needed a valet most urgently. How hard would it be to transform herself into a gentleman? If she acted fast, possibly she could sell the necklace she wore, it had two strings of natural pearls and a ruby clasp. It would fetch her at least two hundred pounds. With that money, she could find safe lodgings in a hotel after making some necessary purchases. In fact, she could travel about for the next two months until she was of age with that amount. But, even if she were to disguise herself as a man, such an undertaking would be too dangerous, far more so than the alternative.

She lifted a hand to her hair, a bite of regret curling through her. The most tremendous loss would be of her heavy dark tresses. Unless it could be tamed, and a wig fitted. Hope and excitement unfurled through Juliana, and she quickened her pace, intending to visit High Holborn and search for a reputable jeweler's store.

Her form had always been petite, her feminine curves almost nonexistent. Her mother had often gently reassured Juliana she was simply a late bloomer. But a couple of years ago, she had accepted her body was not the type to bloom. Once in trousers and the full ensemble of men's clothes, it should be easy to pretend to be a man and work in the earl's home.

Valets did not wear the house livery but dressed as a gentleman. She wouldn't be an ordinary servant, reporting to the butler or the housekeeper, Juliana would be answerable only to the earl. And if his nose were continually in a book, that would be perfect! Considering the delicate nature of womanhood, there should be enough privacy for her ruse to be successful, since in the domestic quarters she would have a room of her own.

Juliana recalled her stepfather's manservant's duties—his most important occupation had been to ensure his master appeared to the best advantage. She had always been reasonably independent and so could iron and repair her own clothes. On occasion, she had even polished her own boots. Though that was only to cover up her unchaperoned escapades into the woods of their Hertfordshire estate, avoiding the stifling expectations of her mother and stepfather. Not having to explain away the mud had been the simplest way to avert being rebuked for behaving in an unladylike manner.

As his valet, she would be responsible for ensuring the earl was well-dressed and immaculate. Would he need her to shave him? Juliana had shaved her father many times before he died when his hands had shaken a little.

I am not an expert at it, but I think I could manage. The very notion of assisting the earl in that manner felt rather intimate. Juliana felt a little unsure if her knowledge was sufficient. A moment of panic almost overwhelmed her senses. What did she know of men's clothes? And what if she were not convincing enough to be hired?

Stop it, she fiercely reminded herself. *I am smart. There is nothing I cannot learn.*

Perhaps with ingenuity for two months, Lord Rawlings's country home could be her refuge.

Good heavens, am I daring to be so scandalous?

She took a deep breath to calm her suddenly pounding heart. A trip to a jeweler was the first business she had to tackle, and she had enough money for a hackney.

Juliana was lucky to find a hackney shortly after, and even in her less than pristine state, the cabbie was pleased to take the fare. Soon she was bowling along in a warm but rather musty cab, which smelled of tobacco smoke and Macassar oil. It was to be expected, as most men used it to dress their hair. It was a familiar scent, but it reminded her that it was a man's world, even in these modern days. Independent women were still frowned upon and considered fast and unconventional.

She put those thoughts to one side as the cabbie pulled his horse to a halt. She paid him what he asked and added an extra coin in thanks. The umbrella and her small reticule being her only luggage, that would have to be rectified. No hotel would accept even a young man without baggage. Juliana strolled along, examining each jewelers' shop she passed on her way. She was wary, especially as passersby were staring at her hair, as she had left her bonnet at Lord Prendergast's. She avoided the busiest of the shops, not wanting to be recognized, even though knowing that was unlikely.

Finally, she found a jeweler that did not seem too fashionable. Her necklace had no particular associations to her, and when she received her inheritance, it could be replaced for another more to her taste. The avuncular proprietor offered what Juliana considered a fair price.

Juliana left with a crisp fold of banknotes that she carefully tucked into her reticule.

Hailing another cab, she asked the driver to head for Wentworth Street, where a street market known as 'Petticoat Lane' was long established. She had considered risking Covent Garden Market, which was considerably nearer. But the area was notorious for the many bawdy houses surrounding the market. An attractive young woman with her hair uncovered, and no maid in tow was guaranteed to get offers that were not respectable. It was safer, by far, to travel further and hope she would not be accosted before she could change her clothing.

Juliana was hungry again by the time she reached the market. Still, her first purchases were a plain bonnet, which she donned, and a small, used leather case to put her purchases in. Only then did she risk buying a paper of hot chestnuts to consume, and she delighted in their warm, nutty flavor, after moving to the side of the street. The market was very littered, but she placed the used paper and chestnut shells in her bag, straightened her back, and placed a slight smile on her face. She toned down her more upper-class speech to sound more like the Cockney accent, hoping that it would assume her strange requests for male clothes for some theatrical performance.

She located most of what she needed on an elderly Jew's used clothing stall. He was polite and allowed her to try the clothes for length and fit against her, and the prices were reasonable. Shirts, cravats, socks, nightshirts, plain blue waistcoats, black jackets, and trousers were all found that looked like they would fit and looked respectable, but not those from an expensive tailor. He also provided her with a warm coat, with a mere two capes, which although a little long, she could adjust.

"Do you know where in the market, I can purchase shoes, a hat, and some new small clothes?" she asked politely.

He gave her several recommendations that would simplify the search. After a little haggling over the cost, he packed the new but second-hand clothes into her bag and promised to dispose of the chestnut paper in the sack he kept for rubbish underneath his stall.

While finding the right stalls, she also bought some linen, polish brushes, and sewing paraphernalia. The other items were soon found, and the wig was purchased in a nearby shop, where a curtained-off area had been arranged for customers' privacy. The barber was prepared to guard the curtain while she changed out of her dress, which she turned inward, so its dampness did not damage her purchases. She would try to dry it and repair any damage when she found a hotel.

The barber was unquestioning about tightly arranging her dark tresses under a short blond wig, which she admitted changed her appearance dramatically. With her new beaver on top and carefully lengthening her stride, she felt her transformation might be accepted. She paid the wigmaker and headed off to find a small hotel for the night with a smile on her face and determination in her heart.

Tomorrow Julian Pryce would offer his services as a valet for hire.

CHAPTER 2

Norbrook Park

The shapely, lush derriere arched in front of Wentworth Alexander Nelson, the Earl of Rawlings, arrested his attention wholly and stirred senses that had been dormant… for well, several months. He could not recall if his baser feelings had ever been so violently awakened to life. The very notion was laughable, improbable, bewildering, and arousing. Wentworth was a man of science. Nothing so base as a well-rounded and delectably formed arse, should have wrenched his thoughts from the mathematical principle he had been mulling over since yesterday.

But this derriere had most certainly distracted his thoughts… and had done so effortlessly. For he could not even recall the hypothesis that had propelled him to the library for long hours after dinner, and now to his room with *A Treatise on Plane and Spherical Trigonometry* clutched in his hand. Wentworth had planned to keep reading, and only when his lids opened no longer would he allow himself to tumble into a deep sleep.

Once the shock of his baser urges acting so strangely passed, he recognized something far worse. He was singularly attracted to his valet's backside! Wentworth never thought he liked his own sex, simply for the fact he'd had over three lovers in his seven and twenty years on earth. And they had all been women. He slowly lowered the mathematical tome on the side table beside his bed and frowned.

His manservant had tugged his boots off and bent over to set them inside the large armoire. Wentworth's pandering gaze had inadvertently been snagged by a gently arched back, a lushly rounded arse, and symmetrically flared hips. *Sweet Mercy.* Wentworth's cock twitched, an ache settled low in his gut, and he gripped the edge of his bed. A choking sound came from him, and he had to slap his chest twice to get himself under control.

"Jeffers," he said abruptly, hoping to get the man's attention. Hoping his valet would forget the damn boots, stand up and face him. It worked. The shoes abandoned, his valet stood and turned to him.

His heart jolted violently. For the second time that night, Wentworth was rendered speechless. He had never seen such beautiful eyes in all his years. They weren't blue. He would have to conduct an experiment to see which pigments could be mixed to produce a color of such arresting beauty. His valet's eyes were dark lavender fringed with long, black lashes.

"Good God, you're not Jeffers," Wentworth snapped, surging to his feet.

And to think this boy had just tugged the boots from his feet and he hadn't even noticed. The lad was short, the top of his head barely in line with Wentworth's chin. The valet he was used to, was of a similar height as Wentworth, had brown eyes, and had kept his gaze respectfully lowered. This one tipped his head and stared at Wentworth a bit too boldly.

"Jeffers is not here, my lord," the young man murmured, low and husky. "His mother took to her sickbed, and the reports from the doctors were dire. Jeffers traveled to Cornwall for the last week, my lord."

A week? His heart jerked a few times. "You've been tending me for a week?"

The young man swallowed. "For the last few days, milord. I... they introduced us, my lord, but you were reading a book, and you did not even lift your gaze from the pages."

The tone was almost accusatory. *Bloody hell!* How had he not noticed? Almost a damn week? "Who hired you?"

His valet edged toward the door, eyeing him warily. Wentworth gathered he was startling him with his gruff questions.

"The housekeeper, Mrs. Dawson, milord."

That was his new housekeeper in Town.

"Mrs. Dawson sent me down with a letter which I presented to the butler of Norbrook Park."

Wentworth frowned. "What is your name?"

"Julian... Pryce, Sir."

The boy was nervous, for he worked his bottom lip, and Wentworth noticed their sensual lushness. That tingle low in his groin became more pronounced. What in God's name was this? He took a steady breath and slowly released it. "How old are you, boy?"

A small rounded chin, absent of any hair, lifted. "Four and twenty, milord. I'll be five and twenty in a few weeks."

That surely must be a fib. The lad looked no more than sixteen years of age. He was very slim. His clothes, while fitted, still gave the impression that they swallowed his frame. The only thing that seemed… a handful was the boy's arse. It had been high and well-rounded and would overflow even in his large hands. Wentworth closed his eyes briefly, gritting his teeth in disgust. To be lusting after a servant in his household was reprehensible. "You're fired. I'll have the butler provide you with a month's wage."

Pryce jolted as if he'd been punched, and his eyes widened, clear panic setting in those lovely depths. "My lord! If I have done something wrong, please, my lord, I most sincerely apologize. But I need this post, my lord."

The panic in those words tugged at Wentworth's conscience, and he mentally cursed. It was not the boy's fault that his master's body had been unruly and very ill-disciplined. It was Wentworth's responsibility to ensure nothing untoward happened under his roof with any of his servants.

He still recalled the distaste he'd felt upon encountering his friend, Simon Drake, Viscount Clayton, dallying with his housekeeper. The man had been unapologetic and unconcerned that he took advantage of someone in his employ who, with all probability, feared refusing his advances. He regretted that such relationships or affairs were a common enough occurrence in society. Men of consequence and rank saw nothing wrong with dallying with a maid or footman if they were pretty enough. Not Wentworth. He had never been a libertine, and he was not about to start now.

"Leave my rooms," he clipped. "I am well able to finish my nightly routine. Have someone send up a cup of hot coffee, and the fire needs to be stoked."

His valet hesitated. "Am I… am I still fired, my lord?"

This Julian Pryce had tended him for a few days now, and there hadn't been an issue. Jeffers' skills had been remarkable. As Wentworth had noticed no fault in Pryce's attentions, then he must have been more than acceptable. Jeffers had previously tended to all his needs diligently and meticulously while being practically invisible.

He had found no fault with his clothes these few days, not that Wentworth was a man who noticed these things to his Aunt Millicent's great distress, considering she often lamented that he was a man who lacked a sense of fashion. Wentworth hardly required a valet to assist him in dressing unless he attended a formal event. And he rarely needed assistance to bathe because he would languish in the large copper tub for an hour with a book in his hand.

"You remain hired."

The 'for now' remained unspoken, but it lingered in the air.

His valet hesitated, a raw but unidentifiable emotion flashing across his face. His stance… was one of anger or perhaps frustration or defiance. As if he wanted to say more, much more, but held himself in check. Unexpectedly, a warning kissed over Wentworth's spine, and his suspicions stirred.

"Are you waiting for something, Mr. Pryce?" he asked with cool civility.

The lad bowed. "I bid you good evening, my lord. And thank you for the opportunity to serve you. I'll not disappoint you."

Then he opened the door and slipped away. Wentworth unbuttoned his shirt and stared at the door for quite a long time. His senses were sharp and well-honed, and they had never led him astray. He was simply used to directing them to his studies and whatever problematic question plagued his brain. Yet now they were telling him that something was decidedly odd about his new valet.

Why had he been hired? Wentworth did not concern himself with staffing beyond hiring a competent housekeeper and a butler at his various estates, and where required, a steward. And even then, his Aunt Millicent or mother normally saw to those household recruitments on his behalf.

"There is something odd about him," he said in the dark, testing his concern aloud.

What? He couldn't say, for nothing except his very inappropriate reaction to a well-rounded arse had made itself evident. With a shrug, he dismissed the lad from his thoughts. Almost an hour later, Wentworth closed *A Treatise on Plane and Spherical Trigonometry*. It was pointless to try to keep reading. It was frustrating and embarrassing that his mind kept drifting to Julian Pryce. With a jolting sense of alarm, Wentworth realized for the first time since he became fascinated with mathematics and science, something else had the power to tease at his brain, infuriating and intriguing him in equal measure.

As he lay in the dark, staring up at his ceiling, he acknowledged the question beating at him. Why had he been so singularly attracted to his valet? What did it mean? Was this a onetime occurrence? And what was he going to do about it, should it continue?

Bloody hell!

He pushed to his feet with a silent snarl, removed his nightshirt, and pulled on his trousers and a simple linen shirt. Wentworth made his way from his room and down the winding stairs to the lower floors. A light shone from beneath the library door, and he frowned. Wentworth opened the door and faltered. He scrubbed a hand over his face, then lowered his hand slowly. His valet was there, curled onto the chaise longue by the fire.

Wentworth wasn't certain if he should be amused or outraged.

"You've availed yourself of my library, I see."

The lad squealed and jerked to his feet, his expression one of comical dismay.

"My Lord!"

Wentworth entered the library and closed the door behind him. He noted the nervous swallow of his valet and filed away the reaction.

"I did not mean to intrude—" the man begun.

"No need to proffer an apology, Julian. I admire those who wish to edify their minds through reading. You may make use of the library when not at work."

"Thank you, my lord," he said with a quick bow, bending to pick up the book that had slipped from his nerveless fingers.

It still astonished Wentworth he had not noticed the lad

before. He vaguely recalled Mrs. Dunn, Norbrook Park's housekeeper of twenty years, informing him of his new valet's arrival. Everything else after that was a blur, for the latest papers printed in the British Association for the Advancement of Science had enraptured him.

"I shall leave and—"

"Stay, have a drink with me," Wentworth invited.

"A drink?"

The lad appeared as if he would collapse, and to Wentworth's thinking, that show of anxiety should be investigated.

"Yes. It would not be remiss if you prepared two glasses of brandy."

"Two brandies?"

"Yes. You'll be having one with me."

The lad blinked rapidly. "It is not fitting, my lord!"

Another glare that was far too bold but had Wentworth's curiosity stirring. "If I say it is fitting, then it is," he said.

"You often invite your servants to drink with you, my lord?"

"I believe you are the first, Julian."

His valet's eyes widened, but he seemed to catch himself from protesting. Wentworth padded over to the chaise and picked up the book his valet had been reading. A romance. *Sense and Sensibility* by Jane Austen. Amusement rushed through Wentworth, and he took the glass when Julian brought it over.

"My good man," Wentworth said. "This is an interesting choice of reading material."

What *was* even more interesting was the dusting of

pink that suffused the boy's face. Well, not a boy. He said he was four and twenty.

That stubborn little chin lifted. "Miss Austen is an author I admire for her dry wit and the irreverent way she portrays her heroine. You should try her, my lord."

How interesting. His previous valet wasn't so decided. "Then I shall sit by the fire and you shall read it to me, hmm?"

"My lord?" his valet gasped.

"I cannot sleep," Wentworth said by way of explanation. "And as you are my man, I believe I will prevail upon you to keep my company, Julian. Or would you prefer to play a game of chess?"

He wasn't sure why he offered that option, for it was unlikely his valet knew how to play.

"Chess, my lord," Julian said, moving toward the two chairs and a small spindly table beside the fireplace.

His valet took a sip of his drink and coughed a few times. Wentworth noted the flush on his cheeks grew more pronounced, and he couldn't help noticing just how bloody pretty the boy appeared. Suddenly he wasn't sure if he wanted to stay behind closed doors with his valet, and that very thought was ridiculous! He was not a man ruled by base urges, nor was he undisciplined.

Annoyed beyond measure, Wentworth grabbed the carafe of brandy and joined his valet by the fire.

"Have you played before?" Wentworth asked, sitting down.

"Yes," Julian said. "My father taught me. We…we often played together, my lord."

An odd feeling of kinship surged inside Wentworth,

and he cleared his throat. "My father taught me to play as well."

His valet offered him a quick smile, as if he too acknowledged they shared a similarity. That smile kicked Wentworth in the chest, and his hand tightened on his glass. "Let's play," he said gruffly.

Almost half an hour later, Wentworth laughed, thoroughly delighted. "I believe you might win, my good man."

"Hmm," Julian said, his brows furrowed in concentration. "How surprised you sound. Checkmate, my lord."

"Your father was a brilliant teacher. This is the first time in...I believe ten years another has told me checkmate."

Julian laughed, the sound low and husky, leaning back in his chair.

"Tell me about yourself, Julian," Wentworth invited, leaning back in his chair and taking a healthy swallow of his brandy.

He flustered him, for once again, the lad seemed nervous.

"Who did you work with before coming in my employ?"

"I...I provided Mrs. Dawson with my references, my lord."

"Are you suggesting I ask my housekeeper? Shall I summon her from London then?"

His valet swiped up his glass of brandy and took a careful sip.

"I worked within Lord and Lady Emerson's household."

Wentworth was familiar with the viscount and his lady. They also had a daughter of marriageable age who often made a cake of herself over the eligible gentlemen of society.

"And where are you from? You have a unique accent, but I cannot quite place it."

Julian's eyes widened. "You have a keen ear, my lord. My mother often told me I sound like any other of the Queen's subjects. I spent my early years in New York in America. I… we made our home in England four years ago after my father passed, and my mother returned to her birth land."

A flash of pain crossed his features before his expression smoothed.

"You have my deepest sympathies, Julian. I know the pain of losing a parent."

His valet made no reply, but glanced at the clock on the mantle.

"I fear I must go, my lord. I have an early morning, and it is already well past midnight."

"You have my permission to sleep in."

His valet looked as if he would swoon.

"I wouldn't dare, my lord!"

"You are dismissed for the night," Wentworth murmured, refilling his glass and lifting it to his mouth.

A soft, relieved sigh slipped from Julian, and he hurriedly stood, bowed, and scampered from the room. At the edge of the threshold, he looked back, and their gazes collided. Wentworth smiled and lifted his glass.

"Sleep well, Julian."

And to his amusement, his valet quickly closed the door as if he were locking the devil inside.

How singularly intriguing.

❧

JULIANA DROPPED her forehead against the large oak door she had just closed. Her heart was a pounding mess, and her knees were weak. It was more than that; Juliana swore butterflies wreaked havoc with her stomach.

The incredible sensual beauty of his smile struck Juliana. It appalled her that she had noticed. The earl was shockingly handsome with his high-sculpted cheekbones, a strong patrician nose, and a full, sensual mouth. Even the wire-rimmed spectacles he wore when reading, only added to his unusual appeal.

He wasn't handsome in the soft manner or anything like the elegant men of society. He was all hard edges and so compelling she'd stared helplessly the first few times she attended to his needs. Yet he hadn't noticed her distraction because he was always reading a book or some journal. It was poorly done of her, but whenever her brother talked about the earl's love of mathematics and his brilliance, she had always imagined someone short, rotund even, with a pair of spectacles perched on a long nose.

The spectacles were about the only things she got right.

"Who cares if he is terribly handsome? This is most certainly not why I am here," she reminded herself softly. "Oh, God, why did you notice me?"

Lords and ladies of society did not take note of their

servants, and this lord did not seem any different. She had quaked in her boots the very first time she had helped him tie a cravat, but the earl hadn't deigned to glance at her. His eyes had been fixed on some point beyond her, and that suited her purpose well.

Since living with her stepfather, she had learned that servants were not seen or heard. They moved about their employers' homes like little elves, working their magic in keeping the mansion cleaned, food ready, clothes laundered and pressed, and always at the beck and call of their mistresses and masters. No matter the hour of the night, her stepfather, and his son, only had to ring a bell and someone would appear, desperately trying not to appear sleepy for fear of being scolded.

Juliana had used all of that knowledge to her advantage, and everything had been going well. Then a few hours ago, in his chamber, she had seen a revelation on his face. Something about her had rattled him…and there had been another emotion in his eyes that had sent her heart surging with alarm.

How frightening and strangely thrilling the entire encounter had seemed to Juliana's overwrought nerves. And then in the library just now! How shocking it had been for the earl to invite her to drink and play chess with him! As if they were acquaintances of similar rank. So many people wouldn't have deigned to lower themselves to drink with people of a class they considered beneath their own.

Her nerves had almost shattered during their interlude in the library. Despite her nonexistent charms, she had wrapped her breasts with linen and cut her waist-length hair to make it easier to fit a wig. Yet the earl's probing stare had been frightening. Almost as if he could see through her, see that she was a lady.

She wondered what thoughts robbed him of sleep and hoped the earl demanding her company, late at night would not be a frequent occurrence. Despite his assurance she could sleep late, Juliana wouldn't dare. This job was too important to her for any missteps.

"Enough," she muttered, thoroughly aggrieved.

Juliana pushed away from the door and hurried toward the servant's quarters. The rest of the house slept, and she made her way up the winding staircase and to her small chamber that was comfortable.

She closed the door behind her and removed her male clothes. With a sigh of relief, she undid the bindings, opened her small armoire, and took out her nightshirt. Once clothed, she slipped beneath the sheets and turned onto her side.

Why did you notice me?

It was then she acknowledged the grave disquiet sitting in her belly. What if the Earl suspected her identity? Surely he would have booted her out of his house or have her arrested for fraud?

"He did fire me," she muttered, turning onto her other side. "*But* I am still here."

Perhaps there was nothing to worry about, and she only needed to ensure her duties were executed well. "I am simply to be his personal attendant for the next seven weeks. I'll ensure his clothes are impeccable, clean his boots, run the water for his bath, put out his clothes for dressing, shave him if necessary, assist him in dressing when required, and pack and unpack his clothes when he travels. Also, load his rifle whenever he goes shooting or hunting, stand behind his chair at dinner, breakfast and luncheon!" Juliana huffed out a groan. "How am I to last for seven more weeks?"

Bloody hell!

CHAPTER 3

A few hours later, Juliana trudged up the servant's staircase of the palatial country house, breathless from the exercise. A pretty maid with curly blonde hair under a lacy cap and large gray eyes, deliberately rubbed her hips against Juliana's as she passed her.

"Mornin' Julian," she said a bit breathlessly. "I didn't see you at supper last night!"

"I was reading," Juliana mumbled, averting her stare from the girl's flirtation and continuing her trek. *And playing chess, drinking brandy, and trying not to ogle the earl.*

"I know I am not supposed to have followers, but...I *like* you, Julian. Tomorrow is my off day, would ye like to take a stroll with me in the village," she said expectantly.

She was gorgeous and playing a game Juliana did not have the time for. "Look...Molly—"

"It's Mary!"

Juliana stared at her for a few seconds until the girl fidgeted. "Mary, I cannot walk with you. You should ask Thomas." That footman seemed madly in love with the girl, bringing her flowers and other trifles at least twice a day.

"What do I want to be asking him for?" she said with a pout and flounced away down the stairs.

With a sigh, Juliana continued toward the first-floor landing. She had been hiding in the earl's country home for six days and was already mixed up in some love affair. Thomas made calf eyes at Mary, who seemed determined to flirt with Juliana. Pretending to be a servant had been a mad scheme born of desperation, and a stroke of genius, but it had its complications.

Juliana was panting by the time she reached the third floor to the earl's chamber. The earl's palatial rooms comprised a large private sitting room, bedroom, dressing room, and a bath chamber. She did not enter right away, but took a few moments to compose her nerves. This she had to do each morning to prepare herself to interact with him, so as not to betray her disguise.

She opened the door and padded inside. The fire did not need to be stoked, so she walked over to the windows. Juliana tugged open the large blue drapes, glancing at the overcast sky. It would be another hour before the earl rose, and the orders she had been given on her first day was that the earl should always awake to see the breaking day. No such luck for him today. It seemed as if it would rain again this morning.

His soft snoring sounded behind her, so she moved carefully, not wanting to disturb his slumber. Stifling an indelicate yawn, she went about her duties with grim efficiency, feeling as if a valet were the worst position she could have filled in this household. She had always been an early riser, enjoying riding before the sun peaked. However, valets were required to awaken at the unholy hour of five in the morning, to ensure their master's day started right.

A soft snort escaped her as she removed from the armoire the earl's clothes for the day. She selected a superfine dark blue jacket, tan trousers, white shirt, socks, neck cloth, and shoes she'd polished during the previous evening. Juliana then hung his apparel upon a stand. She quickly went to the bath chamber for hot water for the earl to shave away his morning stubble. Thankfully, he did that himself, even though it was one duty she would be sure to perform well. A wistful ache went through her heart at the memory of helping her papa shave many mornings.

Her papa hadn't used a valet. Either Juliana or her mama would assist him in shaving or tying a neck cloth if needed. Mostly it had been her mother who would steal quick kisses while she fixed his cravats. That warm recollection had her smiling genuinely for the first time in weeks.

Hurrying toward the door, she faltered when a voice drawled, "A minute, Julian."

Juliana froze. When the butler had given her the list of 'to-dos and don'ts' at the very top had been to leave the earl's chamber after setting out his clothes. This would be the very first morning he roused while she was still there. She gripped the doorknob, her heart pounding. "Yes, my lord?"

Arghh! Why was there a squeak in her voice? Juliana cleared her throat and slowly turned around. The earl was sitting at the edge of his bed, and his chest was bared.

Her entire face flamed, and her heart clamored

erratically. *Do not be silly!*

Thankfully, a sheet was draped across his hips and hanged down to the floor.

When she had entered the house a week ago, she had been desperately afraid the man would take one look at her and knew her to be a lady! But he had been just like her stepfather, looking through her or past her. Yet, Juliana realized it was not because he thought her so inferior to his station, and she did not deserve the honor of his direct stare. The man was simply too preoccupied with whatever was going on in his head.

Except last night when he had stared at her, assessing her with his piercing light brown eyes and overly direct stare, and he was doing it again.

What do you see?

She ruthlessly repressed the need to check if the wig was affixed correctly on her head.

"I have a task for you this morning."

"Yes, my lord?"

"I am bidding a lady friend goodbye. An appropriate gift is in order, I believe."

Juliana blinked. "And what do you require of me, exactly, milord?"

The earl arched a brow, and she silently winced.

"To procure that gift."

"And what should I get?"

The earl scowled. "That is why it is *your* task, Julian."

Valets' duties extended beyond what she understood. Clearly, she was expected to know his preferences for gifts for his lady loves.

"I will make my way to the village as soon as possible,

my lord."

"There is a local jeweler. He is exceptionally good and designs pieces for some top London stores. Mr. Marcus Reed."

"Yes, my lord." Julianna bowed and quickly closed the door behind her.

Returning below stairs, she did her best to avoid a scowling Thomas and a flirtatious Mary. Juliana went into the servants' parlor, where the cook had laid out breakfast on a side table. She quickly filled her plate with eggs, strips of bacon, and round yellow muffins that smelled like cinnamon.

She tried her best not to talk to any of the other servants and kept her head down while she ate. It was not an easy task to keep her voice low and husky. The less she spoke, the better to maintain her ruse. Laughter and chatter swirled around her as many of the staff ate. A few aimed stares at her, but no one attempted to involve her in their conversation.

Juliana was grateful for it, yet even as she listened to them, loneliness pierced her. The housekeeper, Mrs. Dunn, was like a mother hen, asking about their families and always steering the conversation to ensure it remained pleasant and jovial.

Juliana recalled the last time her family had indulged in such warm happiness had been when papa had been alive. Dinner was always informal with papa. He laughed and lived boisterously, having never given many thoughts to the concept of propriety. It wasn't like that in the Viscount's home at all. And while Juliana hadn't hated it, there had been far less laughter and joy at the table.

Shrugging aside the memories that only created this deep ache in her heart, she finished her breakfast. Soon she would have to buy a gift for the earl's mistress. *No, his ex-mistress, that relationship would cease to exist.* She wouldn't examine too much why the notion cheered her, and Juliana finished her meal with a smile in her heart and on her lips.

ALMOST FOUR HOURS LATER, Juliana hopped down from the earl's carriage and walked up the gravel lined driveway to the side door. There was another carriage in the driveway, and the horses and coach were being led by the stable lad to the stable block.

Gripping the parcel, she hurried inside and made her way down the hallway to the earl's study. Surely he would wish to see the gift she had procured on his behalf right away. She knocked on his door, and a very aggrieved voice bid her enter. Twisting the knob, Juliana opened the door and faltered.

An incredibly beautiful lady draped in a yellow gown reposed on the chaise longue, her position designed to tempt any man to admire her charms. The gown was expensive and more suited for an evening occasion, with the new three-quarter length sleeves edged in Brussels lace, leaving her shoulders bared. The front of her skirt revealed a much ruffled and embroidered golden silk under-skirt. Her waist had been tightly corseted as she was breathing fast and shallow. Her décolletage was indecently lowered, and with a gasp, Juliana swore she saw the outline of the lady's nipples.

She quickly averted her gaze to see the earl looking at

her. His mouth twitched, and with a jolt of discomfiture, she realized he was amused, clearly at her. And any red-blooded male would ogle the delightful display.

"Pardon me for interrupting, my lord. I did not know you were occupied."

"You interrupt nothing. Lady Wimpole was just about to leave."

At that announcement, the lady cried prettily in her handkerchief.

For a moment, the earl looked entirely bemused.

"My good lad, do you have the gift?"

The lady perked up at that, delicately dabbing her eyes. "Oh, Wentworth!" she said breathlessly. "No gift will soothe my heart. It is not pretty baubles I want, but you!"

Juliana walked over and handed him the slim box wrapped in pastel-colored paper and ribbons.

"Sophia, you must stop crying," the earl said, exasperated.

"My darling, my nerves have been overset since I got your note," she dramatically cried, pressing her hands to her overflowing bosom. "Wentworth, please, you must not be so heartless!"

"I am sure I sent more than a note. Did you not get a draft of two thousand pounds?"

Juliana inched her way to the door, shamelessly content with watching the tableau unfold.

The earl stood, went over to Lady Wimpole, and handed her the package. She sniffed and took it, opening it, then gasped.

"Oh, Wentworth, this is so lovely."

He made a non-committal sound. "I must get back to my work."

Fat drops of tears rolled down her rosy cheeks. "Why must we be over?" she prettily pleaded.

He stooped to his haunches, his expression softening a bit. "Come now, Sophia, my dear, you are a passionate woman who deserves much more than my infrequent attentions. You've been my mistress for over a year now, and I cannot recall if I've taken you to my bed."

Juliana's heart jolted, and her curiosity about the earl soared. A mistress he had never taken to his bed.

An outraged squawk came from Sophia, and she lurched to her feet, objecting most fiercely to say, "Yes! At least three times…and my darling, how wonderful it was. Surely, you *must* remember."

The earl stood, his mouth parted, then snapped shut. His eyes lit up with a revelation, and he snapped his fingers together. "By God, I've solved the equation! How simple it is, how did I ever miss it?"

Juliana choked on her startled laugh as he made a beeline from the room to his library.

"Well!" Sophia said, flinging herself onto the sofa.

The tears dried, and Lady Sophia pouted and squared her shoulders.

"Would you like some refreshments, madam?" Juliana politely queried.

With a gasp, Sophia looked up, clearly surprised to note Juliana was still in the room. These people really believed servants were invisible. Sophia refused all refreshments, and after fidgeting and sniffling for over an hour, she ordered her carriage around, then left in a flounce. As the room contained many valuable antiques, Juliana had waited for the earl's ex-mistress to depart. In case she was light-fingered in addition to being light with her skirts.

Amused by the entire thing, Juliana had the cook prepare a tray for the earl when he did not come out from the library after a few hours. She opened the door, balancing the tray which held slices of roasted beef, duchesse potatoes, mushrooms which the earl was partial to, cauliflower and a piece of the cook's apple pie with cream to follow, and a bottle of claret.

The earl was bent over his desk, writing in a large leather-bound book. She found a place on his desk to rest the tray, and even with the most mouthwatering flavors filling the room, he did not lift his head.

"I've brought you something to eat, my lord."

He did not glance at her, but his stomach grumbled loudly.

"Let my solicitors know they are to let the Kensington townhouse for Lady Sophia Wimpole for the rest of the year to soothe her offended pride," he said absentmindedly.

"Yes, my lord." Juliana went into her inner jacket pocket, removed the small notebook and pencil she hid there, and made the note.

After, she stood there, staring down at him, an odd feeling stirring inside. It was unfamiliar, and she did not know what to make of it.

He was different from what she had envisioned, and she found herself terribly curious about him. Still, it would be best not to linger in his presence.

CHAPTER 4

Wentworth groaned as he lifted his head and lowered his quill. The fundamental theorems of calculus had always been a favorite of his. Since last week, he had been working on a set of differential calculus questions, and one had given him pause. He relished the challenge of solving complex mathematical equations, and just now, a spark had been lit in his brain, and he realized he had been applying a principle wrong.

Rubbing the back of his neck, he frowned upon seeing that the time was almost seven in the evening, and dusk had fallen. The door eased open, and his valet entered with another tray in his hand. Wentworth glanced around, certain his man had brought him another tray earlier, but his desk was clean.

"You've stopped working, my lord," the lad said, coming over with a tray that smelled divine.

When Julian lowered it onto the desk, Wentworth arched a brow.

"Did the cook know I was working on a problem?"

"Yes, my lord, I informed the kitchens earlier."

"And they still prepared this feast?"

His valet wrinkled his nose most charmingly. "I was instructed on my first day to always alert the cook whenever you have shut yourself away to work. Today was the first day I witnessed it, my lord."

"That does not explain all this loveliness," he said, taking up the knife and cutting into the breast of a roasted quail. Wentworth groaned at the first taste. He was hungrier than he'd realized.

"I ordered the kitchens to prepare something proper, my lord. With all the energy you expend to work, a few cakes and sandwiches would not do."

Wentworth froze and glanced up into the flushed face of his valet. "How novel," he murmured. "I shall not complain about you overriding my order, for this meal is beyond delicious. So, my good lad, thank you for being thoughtful."

Wentworth had informed his kitchens years ago that whenever he is consumed with a problem or something new, the cook could forgo the three to five-course dinner she prepared. Even when she did something simple, the tray would often be removed untouched.

"Request a second tray from the kitchens, Julian. I want the same things I have here and in the same quantity."

"Yes, my lord," he said and hurried from the room.

Wentworth took his tray over to the table by the fire and slowly savored the thyme-infused quail until Julian returned with another tray.

"Please set it down over here."

His valet complied, setting down another tray with half a roasted quail, slices of roast pork, vegetables, delicate chicken-filled pastries, and fish in crème sauce. There was spiced cake, wine, and fruit compote in an elegant jelly.

"I will retire my lord and—"

"Nonsense. Join me. The second tray is for you. I find I do not wish to dine alone tonight, and who better to join me?" Wentworth smiled. "I haven't suggested that you kill someone, Julian, stop looking at the door with that air of desperation."

A choking sound came from his valet before his slim shoulders squared, but most importantly, his stomach rumbled.

"It seems you've not had supper either, and if I am to guess correctly, that is at least another hour away. Now, join me."

He sat, his throat working a nervous swallow.

Wentworth cut into a buttered golden potato. "Do I make you nervous, Julian?"

He scoffed and lowered himself in the chair. "Of course not, my lord."

Wentworth poured a generous amount of brandy into two glasses and handed one to his valet.

"I should be the one serving you, my lord," he mumbled, taking the glass and a sip of the golden liquid.

Wentworth couldn't explain why he liked his valet's company. There was an air of something mysterious about him, and the suspicion Wentworth had felt about his valet still lingered.

"Is it true that you graduated from Oxford University at seventeen?" Julian asked.

The question was unexpected, but it showed the lad was also curious about him.

"Yes. It took some finessing from my father for me to gain admittance at thirteen. But a demonstration of my ability opened the doors."

His valet popped a piece of roasted quail in his mouth and chewed thoughtfully. "What was it like? Attending that important university at such a young age?"

"Lonely," Wentworth replied without thinking. "That came out without me giving your question much thought."

"But I believe it an honest response, my lord, thank you," he said with a soft smile.

Wentworth barely contained his flinch. Bloody hell, that sweet curve of lush lips wreaked havoc with his damn heart. It seemed his infernal attraction to the lad was still there. He knew, of course, there were men and women who were attracted to both sexes, but the notion that he too had such a sexual interest was befuddling to his senses.

"Why was it lonely?"

Wentworth lowered his knife and fork and reached for his brandy, which he finished in one go. "While I was thrilled to be studying advanced mathematics and the various sciences, I was still a thirteen-year-old lad who, at times, hungered to play. The older boys did not understand me, nor did they attempt to befriend me or respond to my overtures. I spent most of my time studying or reading in my room or taking long walks by the river."

He noted with some amusement that for such a petite lad, his valet had a healthy appetite. The tray was already half gone. Grabbing the decanter, the earl topped up his glass.

They ate and drank in a silence that felt almost companionable. Wentworth noted the lad kept his eyes lowered, and whenever their gazes met, the lad would hurriedly look away. Sometimes he would bite his lower lip, and at other times he would blush.

The suspicion which had flowered inside him spun on its axis to something different. The more he stared at his valet, truly stared, the prettier the man became. Instead of looking away, which he had always done to deny the attraction, Wentworth examined his face with exquisite thoroughness.

The slope of his valet's jawline seemed almost delicate. He doubted he shaved. The curl of his short blond hair across his forehead gave him a distinctly softened air, almost feminine. Something about his hair did not fit with his eyes or the sun-kissed tone of his complexion. His valet possessed a beautiful heart-shaped face, an upturned nose, and a very kissable cupid's bow mouth.

He flushed upon noticing Wentworth's regard.

"My lord, you are staring—"

A hiccup stopped the rest of his words, and he giggled. Wentworth straightened in his seat when his valet glared at the decanter of brandy.

"What sorcery is this?" he muttered, befuddled.

"You are not used to drinking," Wentworth drawled.

"I…ah…I only indulged because you invited me to, my lord." Then he smiled again. Except, this time, it was different. This smile was brighter, wider, without a hint of reserve. And even more interesting, his entire face glowed with the beauty of that smile.

Wentworth's heart jerked as the most improbable idea

teased his thoughts. Not very gentlemanly of him, but he refilled the lad's glass for a third time. "Come, drink with me."

"I really should go...and...go and prepare your bath," his valet replied through a series of hiccups. Despite that protest, he reached for the drink and took a few healthy swallows. "I think they've stopped," he said with a sigh of relief.

The lad pushed back his chair, stood, and wobbled. Wentworth surged to his feet and grabbed him about the shoulders to steady him. His valet peered up at him, and in his eyes, Wentworth saw an awareness, a touch of desire.

Wentworth released him as if he'd been burned. "Go," he said from between clenched teeth. "No need to prepare a bath, and I do not need help to undress."

The lad nodded, but he did not move. Instead, he sighed gustily. "I feel warm...and shivery. It is the oddest thing. I feel it every time I look at you." He looked so young and vulnerable at that shocking confession.

"You are tipsy," Wentworth said.

He made a soft, noncommittal sound. Julian lifted a hand and cupped Wentworth's jaw. They both froze at the remarkable intimacy.

"You are so very handsome," he whispered. "I should not notice it...I *dare* not notice it, but it seems I cannot help it."

"Why do you not dare?" Wentworth demanded gruffly, feeling a bounder for taking advantage of the lad's state. But how else could he assuage his curiosity when his valet was so forward?

"Because you are my employer, and such wayward

thoughts might compromise my ruse."

Good God. "What ruse?"

"I…" Alarm chased across his face. "I…I feel…" He paused and yawned widely. "I believe I need to get into bed."

Wentworth gripped the lad's hand, removed it from his face, and caught sight of the neatly manicured fingertips. The feel of his valet's hand was soft and…bloody hell.

His valet was a woman. Wentworth did his best to hide the shock blasting through him.

Julian turned around and swayed, and Wentworth caught him and swung him into his arms.

"I feel like I am floating," a soft voice said.

Sweet Mercy. The weight in his arms felt right…felt arousing.

He hesitated. To carry him like this up the servant stairs would have their tongues wagging for weeks and might make life uncomfortable for his valet for quite some time. Swiftly deciding, Wentworth left the study and made his way up the stairs to his chamber.

Once in his rooms, he lowered his valet in the center of his bed. A sigh of great comfort slipped from him…her, and she promptly fell asleep. Wentworth stared down at the creature before him, wondering if he was going mad. It was such a wild supposition to make. A lady disguised as a man and working as a valet. Utterly preposterous. Yet his thoughts would not move on from the idea.

His valet's speech suggested a man educated, but most manservants had adequate reading and writing skills. Pryce seemed too nervous around him. And that stroke against his jaw, it had hinted at a longing, of want.

"Perhaps I am going mad," he muttered, cross with himself. It had been a simple touch to his face, how in God's name did he decipher so much from that caress. "But a lady in the guise of a man would indeed add up to a ruse worth protecting."

Peering down at the body on his bed, he detected no womanly shape. Bindings were not miraculous cloths. He sat on the edge of the bed and slowly undid the neck cloth. Wentworth allowed his fingers to tease at the buttons, battling the urge to undo them.

To take such advantage of his valet felt wrong, yet curiosity beat at him in unrelenting waves. He touched Julian's chin, noting the soft, silky texture of his valet's skin.

What if I should undo these buttons and find a woman...what would I do? A hot, urgent feeling coiled low in his gut, and he released a shaky breath. Bloody hell, his thoughts and urges were that of a damn scoundrel.

His valet batted his hand away and muttered, turning onto his side. Wentworth sighed. He had never behaved in an ungentlemanly fashion before. But he was tempted to do so now by rolling Julian over and removing his neck cloth and shirt to reveal what was underneath.

Surely, there were other methods for finding out if his valet was really a woman pretending to be a gentleman? A burst of thrill went through him, and he stood and walked over to the small writing table and chair near the fire and sat.

Any sort of experiment invigorated Wentworth's blood. Retrieving one of his unused journals, he opened it, dipped the quill into the inkwell, and carefully outlined his research with factual details.

Problem: I find my valet attractive, but I am not bent toward the same sex. His speech is well mannered and eloquent, showing education above that of a valet, and his mannerisms are effeminate.

Hypothesis: The valet is a lady in disguise.

Method: Whether or not in disguise, a lady should not be able to hide her reflex reactions. A campaign to shock the valet's senses will be undertaken while observing her reactions to certain improprieties.

1. *While my valet aids me in my bath, a keen observation must be made when certain areas are being washed.*
2. *I shall engage my valet in conversation regarding the fairer sex.*
3. *I shall attempt to get remarkably close and try to steal a kiss. Any man or boy should recoil.*

Predictions: I expect my valet will heavily blush and avoid eye contact, and faint or flee when faced with touching of any kind with a man. She may also have heavy uncontrolled breathing, an evident blush, and possibly a feminine fragrance when her personal space is invaded.

Analysis: I shall record my observations in a journal entry after each test.

Conclusion: If my valet is not a lady, I shall chalk up my reactions to the man's rear as a lapse in judgment. However, if the man is indeed a woman, the question needs to be answered, why does a lady who seems to bear me no ill will need to disguise herself as my valet? And what am I to do about this stubborn attraction?

CHAPTER 5

J uliana stirred slowly awake, then sharply inhaled with awareness. The earl was in her chamber. She smelled his uniquely masculine fragrance. Juliana shifted, tugging the sheets closer to her nose, and inhaled deeply. She jolted, and her eyes flew open. Her sheets were not this soft and sweetly scented, her mattress was not so comfortable! With a jolting sense of shock, Juliana realized she was in the earl's chamber…and in his bed. She lurched upright, her heart pounding a fierce rhythm.

A quick glance revealed she was still dressed, but her boots had been removed, along with her jacket, and her neck cloth loosened. Oh! She swung her gaze wildly about the room, and then gasped, her hand fluttering to her chest.

"I am in my bathing chamber, Julian," the earl's voice drawled. "And you're to attend to me."

How was this possible? "Why am I in your bed, my lord?"

She swallowed. Her voice had come out as a squeak and not the low husky murmur she practiced.

"You got intoxicated last night. I could not leave you on the floor of the library."

"Drunk?" A vague memory of him inviting her to drink with him floated through her thoughts. She felt a leaden weight settle in her stomach, and Juliana covered her face with her hands. How could she have been so foolish?

"Yes, do you not recall the events of last night?"

The amused, predatory way he said that had her mouth falling open. *Dear God!* Yet she could form no reply.

A splash sounded. *"My good man, my back needs scrubbing."*

She pushed off the bed, grabbing her clothes from the valet stand, and hurriedly rearranged her neck cloth and put on her jacket. "I will be right with you, my lord."

Stooping, Juliana donned her shoes, her mind churning. The earl had never asked her to attend him with his bath before. Why was he doing so now? She knew it was usually the duty of a valet, but he hadn't asked to do so for the last several days.

Did he suspect her?

Do not be silly, she chided herself. *If he had suspected me, the earl would have booted me from his home on my arse, not ordered me to bathe his naked body.*

She hurried to his private bath chamber to find he was immersed in a large and most luxurious tub. The walls and floor were of blue and white marble, and had a sunken bath with spigots for hot and cold running water. The modernization of his manor's bath chamber plumbing saved the maids or his valet from the arduous task of lugging pails of hot water up several flights of stairs.

His hair was wet and curled at his nape. She kept her eyes glued there, overwhelmingly conscious of how alone they were, of how hazardous this situation had become.

He was naked.

"My lord," she began. "The maids who brought up your coffee did they—"

"Your figure in my bed was just a lump under the covers, Julian."

"Where did you sleep, my lord?" She closed her eyes, wanting the ground to part and swallow her. Why did she ask that?

He was silent, and it was as if she could feel his amusement.

"My back," he murmured.

She took the soap and lowered to her knees behind him. Without looking down, she dipped it into the water and then brought it to his shoulders. Juliana rubbed the bar against his skin, creating a gentle lather. Her motions were slow as she carefully soaped the expanse of his shoulders and upper back, which were surprisingly muscular.

He shifted, leaned forward for her to reach his lower back. Her gaze landed on his hands, which gripped each edge of the bath as if they were lifelines.

Did she affect him?

Her heart started to pound, and she rubbed his back as quickly as possible. She took a washrag and repeated her motions, closing her eyes so as not to ogle the golden and muscular expanse of his skin.

"I slept beside you," he unexpectedly murmured. "You are a fascinating sleeper."

She felt her breath catch at his outrageous remark, and

she dropped the soap into the water. Juliana scrambled to her feet, utterly at a loss as to what to say. Then the earl gripped the edges of the tub and hauled himself to his feet.

Juliana almost fainted.

His thighs and calves were thick, his buttocks lean, and his back and shoulders delineated with muscle. Water sluiced off his powerful frame as he stepped from the tub and turned around. The earl seemed oblivious to his nudity, while she experienced an acute awareness of it, of *him*.

Juliana had never seen a naked male body before, except in sculpture and oil paintings. She wanted desperately to look away but could not. The earl…he was a fine specimen. His body was muscled in wonderful proportions, his skin tone even implied he swam outdoors in the nude. The very idea was shocking *and* decadent.

At her mute regard, his sensual mouth curled at one corner. It was a smile…one that was almost a dare, one she wouldn't have associated with the scholarly earl. Juliana belatedly realized the man before her did not resemble a scholar in any way…but more of a libertine bent on seduction.

Suddenly, the air in the room felt too thick, too tension-filled.

Oh, God, does he know I am a girl, or does he also like the same sex?

She wanted to pretend indifference to his charms but couldn't manage it. There was a slight trembling of her body, and her heart pounded so hard. The pit of Juliana's stomach fluttered, and there was a hot, startling ache between her thighs. The response felt strange, primitive, but also right.

"Bring the towel and come here."

That command had her taking a step back, but her damnable curiosity continually betrayed her, and she swept her gaze slowly over his perfectly formed chest and down…a strangled gasp escaped her, and she froze.

His manhood, a thing she had only ever seen in museums, was not so small as those paintings and sculptures implied! And under her gaze, it lengthened and grew fat. Her mouth fell open and a very embarrassed squeak emitted from Juliana.

"My good man, I am frightfully curious about the blush reddening your cheeks," the earl said with mild amusement in his tone.

Oh!

Her gaze snapped up. An expression she had never seen on another heightened the handsome lines of the earl's face. It was intense…and caused her belly to get even hotter. She clasped her cheeks, finding them frightfully heated. Too rattled to proffer any reply, she grabbed the towel tossed over the screen and flung it at him. Then Juliana whirled around and fled from his chamber as if the devil chased her.

Closing the door with a much too hard slam, she leaned against it, her chest lifting with her harsh breathing. Juliana stiffened, wondering if that very sensual and amused laughter from inside the chamber was her imagination.

Good heavens, what does this mean?

Nothing, she scolded herself fiercely.

It was customary for a valet to assist his master in a bath. It was also expected for the valet to towel dry his master if required.

But it is not normal to run away like a frightened rabbit at the sight of a naked man!

She smoothed her features, drawing upon all her resolve to not betray her thoughts or feelings. Reaching deep inside for equanimity, Juliana opened the door and entered the earl's chamber. He had withdrawn from his bath chamber to his sleeping quarters, and the dratted man was still naked! He was slowly toweling his hair, the muscles of his shoulder rippling and twisting.

He turned, an expression of surprise and then admiration lit in his eyes.

"You came back."

"Yes, of course, my lord."

His lips twitched, and his brown eyes grew warm. "I thought you would have run all the way to London, my good lad."

He is still calling me, 'good lad.' That was a good sign. Her shoulders relaxed, and the tight feeling in her belly eased.

"I could only get rid of the bug outside, my lord."

"Ah, it was a bug?"

She lifted her chin. "Of course, why did you think I dashed out so hurriedly."

He arched a brow and looked like he was suppressing laughter. "And what kind was it?"

Annoyed, she briskly said, "I didn't look once I got the critter out of my pants."

The earl laughed, the sound low, husky, and very devilish.

Juliana offered him a bland, and hopefully, professional smile. "I shall dry your back and shoulders if you still wish it, my lord."

"How composed you are," he murmured provokingly. "I believe I have the matter in hand."

Relief swelled inside, but she did her best to not reveal that reaction. "I will lay out your clothes for the day."

Her stomach chose the moment to grumble embarrassingly.

"It is already late. Break your fast."

She hesitated, tempted to stay, and insist on completing her duties, but also understood a lifeline when she saw one. "Since I am not needed, I shall go and have something to eat, my lord."

She bowed and withdrew from the earl's chambers, careful not to appear jittery despite the wild thumping of her heart and her trembling knees.

CHAPTER 6

H is valet really might be a young lady.

On the heels of the very thought, Wentworth's cock surged to life with maddening eagerness. With a silent curse, he tugged on his banyan, uncaring he soaked the material. Wentworth took a few steps toward his door and had to forcefully halt himself. It was madness to even think to chase his servant and question him...her.

He scrubbed a hand over his face. What would he say? Accuse the man of being a lady in disguise? Wentworth had nothing to go on but a few delightful blushes and the raw desire that had flickered in those lovely eyes just now.

In his thoughts, he could no longer think of Julian as a male. It just did not correspond with his visceral desires and imagination.

Do not be so quick to prove your theory, he silently reminded himself.

What if his valet was still a lad in the throes of first passion? *Bloody hell!* Calming his thoughts, he went over to the writing desk in his room and retrieved his journal.

Journal Entry Two

Wentworth stared at the words he wrote, wondering exactly what he should record. The first phase of his experiment had gone really well, and he was fifty percent certain his valet was a lady. When Julian had first run away, Wentworth's certainty had been like an uncrushable rock, but the lad had returned, admirably composed and unflinching.

How brave you are.

A young miss with delicate sensibilities might not have acted with such equanimity after seeing a naked man on the brink of arousal. He closed his eyes against the memory of that gaze caressing over his body, that look of awe, the blush, and heat in those lavender eyes. That primal and genuine reaction, the rise and fall of her chest, that tight swallow, the hard bite on her bottom lip...surely that was the behavior of a person who wanted him. And he, in turn, wanted her, desired her, more than was rational.

Their attraction was decidedly mutual, and he wasn't altogether certain what was his next step. Or why it was even necessary for him to take a step forward. Wentworth did not feel like himself. He was enjoying this little experiment far too much, and it had nothing to do with scientific theories and discovery.

His body and heart screamed irrevocably that Julian was a woman, but his eyes still needed the irrefutable proof. He dipped the quill into the ink and scrawled in his journal.

Observation: My valet was most rattled at my naked body. Julian was hardly able to meet my eyes, and a rosy blush suffused his or perhaps her face. The breathing of my subject also became fast and erratic, and then he/she ran away. That could be considered the response of a very missish young lady with delicate sensibilities. So, if Julian is a female, she is an ingénue, not an accomplished light-skirt seeking to find a wealthy protector.

I wonder if one of my friends has paid her to this imposture, some will find that amusing. They think me too staid and obsessed with my books. It would be like Patrick De Vere to send me a beautiful demi-vierge, just out of pure mischief. However, there was a look of arousal in my valet's eyes, but no understanding or experience was indicated. If she is a would-be courtesan, then she must be an outstanding actress. My valet is more educated than Jeffers or any other valet I have encountered, so why would a young woman of a privileged family risk exposure and her reputation by taking on a male disguise?

I believe my valet was sincere in pleading to not be dismissed from my employment. I got the impression that the prospect of being turned off frightened the valet. So if my valet is a woman, what is she escaping from? That leaves me with the conundrum of my own desires for her and my responsibilities to my employees. I should not seduce an innocent or abandon one to unknown dangers. My desires conflict with my own moral standards, whether my valet is male or female and should be kept in check. The dilemma is stimulating and amusing. Although I should probably pay my valet to leave, I am enjoying his or her company very much.

It is still a possibility that my valet is a boy who is uncomfortable with having sexual preferences for his own sex. I do not wish to believe that conclusion, but if that is the case, I have the option to discourage his advances or sack him.

The subject's return to the chamber immediately following his or her distress showed a temperament capable of rallying swiftly under pressure. It also revealed Julian possessed a mind able to think quickly and who is inventive in tight situations. Indeed, the ruse being discovered would have made it difficult for him or her to return to my chamber because of my behavior, but how Julian governed his or her reaction was admirable.

It is easy to conclude Julian has never seen another naked man. His or her fascination and alarm were too pronounced. This, however, is no conclusive evidence that Julian is a lady. As a young lad, educated at home, seeing the body of another naked male is not guaranteed.

Unexpected outcome: The variable I'd not made allowances for was myself. My reaction to Julian's stare was rather alarming. I cannot recall ever feeling such pleasure at another's admiration before. Not even Lady Sophia, my most recent lover, was able to elicit half of the desire I felt and from a mere stare. My own reactions bear scrutiny, and so do my responses to Julian. Why am I so powerfully attracted? I am not a creature given over to physical desires, yet I cannot help admiring the prettiness of her features or the lushness of her smile. Though I fear I am more attracted to her braveness and her ingenuity in planting herself in my household. The character it reveals is one of strength and of quick wit.

The next phase in my experiment must allow for closer observations of Julian, and I should also undertake a probe into his background. While it would be relatively easy to hire an investigator, I am more interested in uncovering this through conversation. Even the lies he or she will be forced to make will be revealing.

Why? This desire remains unknown to me, but it feels more than mere curiosity.

WENTWORTH LOWERED the quill and closed the journal. A quick glance outside revealed a bright sky, which propelled him to his feet and to the windows. This autumn had been unusually wet, the rain only rarely stopping to allow the sun to emerge. He predicted it might promise a harsh winter, with the possibility of heavy snow. He had missed his morning ride, but he would take advantage of the weather and spend the day outdoors. Possibly do a spot of hunting.

Despite his love of mathematics and reading, he also immensely enjoyed the outdoors and sportsmanship. Wentworth did not bother to ring for further assistance, but quickly dressed and made his way downstairs. It did not escape him that it was several hours since he had paused in reading Sir Isaac Newton's theory on universal gravitation, which had been examined in the third edition of *Mathematical Principles of Natural Philosophy*. Wentworth owned the first edition published in Latin, which he had read in full, but enjoyed reading the differences between the editions and what it revealed about the expansion of knowledge. Knowledge, he had concluded, was exponential and would always grow and transmute to the delight of avid followers of the sciences like himself.

Spending more time with his valet and uncovering Julian's actual character could not wait. He scoffed. It did not escaped Wentworth's attention that he wasn't addressing exactly *why* it was so important.

This is just a diversion, he silently told himself. *One that is merely fun and different.* He had always been the type to enjoy new challenges and unique situations. He reached the landing only to draw up at the sight of his mother—the Dowager Countess of Rawlings, Aunt Millicent—a dowager viscountess, as her late husband had died two years previously, and his two cousins in the hallway. Three footmen were wrestling with their luggage, and his ordinarily unflappable butler gave the impression of being almost harried.

His mother, a woman of renowned energy and gaiety, could have that effect. "Mother?"

The dowager countess glanced up, a radiant smile blooming on her mouth. Wentworth's mother remained quite a beautiful woman at seven and forty, having retained her youthful slenderness and vivacity. Her light brown eyes with striking green flecks at their center, a perfect replica of his own, glowed with warmth and delight.

The countess clapped her gloved hands together. "My darling, Wentworth, how wonderful to see you! I've missed you." She hurried over to him, her arms held wide.

He hugged her to him for a few seconds. "I've missed you too, Mother. I thought you and Aunt Millicent intended to stay in Brighton for the next few weeks." Along with his hoydenish twin cousins who seriously needed correction. However, their over-indulgent mother had spoiled them rotten. The girls were only sixteen years of age and were considered ravishing beauties and heiresses. How his aunt planned to take them in hand when it was time for their debut on the marriage mart, he had no notion, nor did he envy her the task.

His mother took her time examining him, and he mockingly bared his teeth for her inspection. She laughed and quickly hugged him again. "You know when we are apart that I worry about you. That is why I despair of you not finding a wife. You need someone to take care of you."

"I am a grown man with an army of servants," he said drily. "My future countess will not be a caretaker but a helpmate, a lover, a confidant."

A beautiful pair of lavender eyes flashed in his thoughts, and he jolted.

"I am surprised you know it," she said caustically. "Considering you've gone another season with no notable attachment or even the vaguest whispering that you are courting a lady. My son, I declare I would be deliriously happy should I hear your name attached to a scandal."

He grunted softly. "Mother, if you are here to harangue me about marrying again, you must turn right around and head back to Brighton."

Aunt Millicent came over to him in a whirl of petticoats, an overlarge feathered hat which tickled his nose when she enfolded him in a hug.

"Why have you all descended on me?" he muttered with aggrieved fondness.

"Ungrateful child," she said cheerily, kissing his cheek. "Did you not get our letters?"

He vaguely recalled his butler presenting him with some correspondence in her handwriting a few days ago. "I haven't read through them as yet."

"Well, if you did," Henrietta, his spritely cousin, and

the older of the twins said, "You would know mama and Aunt Eleanor are planning a country ball, and it is their intention to hold it here at Norbrook Park in a couple of weeks' time. That, my dear cousin, is why we are here! And to visit you. We all dreadfully missed you."

Isabelle, the younger cousin by only three minutes, winked at him, and Wentworth smiled. He smelled his mother's and aunt's scheme a mile away. If he had not selected a bride from the marriage mart in London, they would cast their net toward the local offerings.

Wentworth was tolerably amused. He would marry when he was ready, and not before. Ignoring his mother's machinations was the best way to get that message across.

"I am heading to do a spot of hunting."

"You've invited a hunting party?"

"No. I am going alone with my valet."

"Hunting alone? Why I've never heard the likes of it," Aunt Millicent said, staring at him.

"We'll have a larger hunting party in a few weeks for mother's annual house party."

His mother beamed. "And I am off to plan these marvelous events with my sister," she said, strolling toward the larger drawing-room.

His aunt and her two troublesome daughters followed, their heads held close, whispering. They aggravated his peace from time to time, but he was happier whenever his family visited. And he might be happier with a wife and children underfoot.

Wentworth frowned, realizing that he'd never given serious consideration to the idea of matrimony in all his seven and twenty years of life. His mother, however, had mentioned it every time she visited him for the last five years. And the topic had held the same importance to him as if she'd mentioned cow dung. He barely paid any attention to her urgings, only knowing he would select a wife from the marriage mart when he was ready.

Perhaps he would have even given cow dung more thought since he'd written a paper once about the importance of fertilization for the growth of certain crops. It wasn't that Wentworth was averse to the state of holy wedlock, for he would eventually marry, as all gentlemen with responsibilities entrusted to them must do.

It just didn't seem essential or currently inspiring, he thought with a jolt.

Julian appeared at the top of the hallway, and Wentworth's mouth dried. His valet had a frown on his face until he glanced up and saw him. His expression changed to one of wary guardedness.

You are most definitely hiding something.

"My good lad, you'll accompany me to do a spot of hunting."

Pleasure lit in his eyes. "Yes, my lord. I shall retrieve the Manton."

"A pair of them. And a burlap sack for the game."

"Do you use hunting dogs to collect the game, my lord?"

"Yes."

"I'll alert the kennel master."

"And the stables."

Julian frowned. "We'll not go on foot, your lordship?"

Though riding on horseback while hunting was usually reserved for foxhunting, those skilled in balance and sight could seat a horse while bird-hunting. And Wentworth was skilled in that regard, and his lands too large to head out on foot. "No. Two horses. You do know how to ride?"

A slight hesitation, then Julian replied, "Yes, my lord."

"Good. I am heading to the dining hall for some breakfast. No need to tend me there. I will meet you in the stable yards in an hour's time."

His valet bobbed and hurried away to do his bidding. At the same time, he made for the dining room, anticipation enlivening his blood. Wentworth wondered what he really anticipated, the thrill of being outdoors hunting, or spending time in his valet's presence.

It being the latter irritated him, for he did not like to invest his time into anything that did not have an endgame. What if he truly proved his valet was a lady? What would he do with the knowledge? If nothing, then he would have wasted considerable time that could have been invested into something more worthwhile that might have an eventual positive outcome. Yet there was a small part of him that genuinely thought there was nothing better that he could do at this time.

Astonishing and preposterous.

CHAPTER 7

J uliana rode her horse with effortless grace, discreetly
admiring the skillful yet elegant way the earl sat upon
his horse. They had entered the deep forest of his
lands over thirty minutes ago, two large dogs bounding
ahead. The earl held a hunting rifle with familiar ease and
skill. She carried the other along with a burlap sack rolled
behind her saddle to keep whatever game he shot down.

She hadn't thought a gentleman so in love with books
would be equally at ease with the outdoors. But she should
have suspected it, given the perfection of his body. He
hadn't been soft anywhere, and the memory of his
masculine nakedness had heat rising in her cheeks.

Do not think of it, Juliana!

His society loved hunting. Once they retired to the
country, they would typically shoot birds and rabbits
during the fall and hunt foxes during the winter. She
understood shooting the birds since they could be eaten,
not so much pursuing the beautiful, furry creatures such as

foxes. She acknowledged that they were a pest to farmers but regretted the brutal manner of their extermination.

The air felt crisp, clear, and chilly. She inhaled it deeply into her lungs. Though she had been in the earl's home a week now, this was the first time she had spent any considerable time outdoors. The rain and the chill of the previous days had been a deterrent to walking during her lunch hour. "What breed are they, my lord?" she asked, staring ahead at the beautiful pair of dogs.

"They are Belvoir hounds."

"And they'll bring back the birds without eating them?"

He flashed her a quick smile. "And without their teeth piercing the bird's feathers and flesh. Ptolemy and Pythagoras are well trained."

He nudged his horse into a trot, and she followed suit, watching the woods. The dogs raced ahead, a sharp bark sounded, and then a flock of pheasant took to the sky. The sudden flapping of their wings sounded loud in the stillness of the forest, and excitement thrummed in her blood.

The earl aimed and without hesitation fired.

"Did you get it?" Juliana asked.

"Of course," he said with a touch of arrogance.

She laughed but hurriedly tempered it from sounding airy. Juliana ended up choking and spluttering.

"Another bug?" the earl drawled mockingly.

His gaze upon her was piercing.

She made the motion of plucking something from her mouth and tossing it to the forest floor. "Why, yes, but it is gone now. Thank you for your concern, my lord. It is positively heartwarming."

He smiled, slow and far too sensual, and she had to avert her gaze.

"I find I am curious about you, Julian. Tell me about yourself," the earl smoothly invited.

His words kicked her in the chest, and her grip reflexively tightened on the reins. "I led a rather boring life, your lordship. There is not much to tell."

"I enjoy boring. Indulge me, my good lad."

My good lad. There was an emphasis on those words which had alarm stirring in her veins. She felt as if he knew something, but surely it couldn't be so. She sent him a challenging stare. "What exactly do you wish to know, my lord?"

Admiration and an indefinable expression darkened his eyes. "Astonish me."

A flock of birds rose in the sky, and acting on the dare in his gaze, she nudged the horse into a small trot, took aim, and shot the bird the farthest in the sky. It tumbled through the air to land in the bushes, and the dogs darted after it.

The earl rode up beside her, and a long whistle of admiration came from him. "Mightily impressive, my good lad! Are we to have a competition?"

She laughed and had to bite into her bottom lip to halt the too feminine sound. "I would thrash you soundly, my lord. It would be unfair."

His eyes widened in mock outrage. "Is that so?"

"Yes." Juliana tossed her head. "My father was an expert hunter and marksman, and he taught me everything he knew about shooting."

"Ah-ha!" He quickly reloaded his rifle. "But can you do this?"

He urged his horse into greater speed, and Juliana raced after him, a thrill bursting in her heart. Without slowing, he aimed his gun and her breath caught at his majesty—the image he presented atop his massive black stallion, his coat flapping behind him, that rifle held so steadily…his form so graceful.

It was impossible for him to shoot anything at such a precarious speed, but he fired, and a pheasant fell from the air. Juliana felt breathless by the time she reached his side.

"Now, can you beat that, my good lad?" he demanded, grinning.

"Ah…why yes, I can."

His smile wiped away, and he narrowed his gaze. "Prove it."

Juliana reloaded her rifle, then surged her horse ahead. He thundered after her, and for several minutes they were caught up in their own world of fun. Thunder rumbled overhead, and she scowled at the sky. "It was too good to last!"

"We might have about an hour or more before the rain starts."

She peered up at the sky beyond the skyline of the towering beech and oak trees. "And how can you tell?"

"The clouds are not yet so swollen or dark. We've ridden a considerable distance from the main house, but you are an expert horse…man. We should make it back before the deluge."

The hunting dogs had gathered the birds in one area, and she admired their skills. Juliana hopped down from the horse to stuff the mix of birds they had taken down, a few quail, pheasant, and even a couple of wild ducks. "We have nineteen birds between the two of us. I shot ten and you nine," she said, grinning up at him.

His brow arched. "*I* am the loser in our impromptu match?"

"Yes, my lord."

"And I suppose you can tell which bird fell from your rifle?"

She swallowed the giggle rising in her throat. "Most assuredly."

He dismounted, loosely holding his horse's rein. "We'll take them to the small church not too far from here. The vicar will see them distributed to the villagers after taking one or two for himself."

"That is very kind of you."

"Well, we cannot eat them all, and I am certain the manor's gamekeeper caught enough fowl today for the kitchens, and hopefully, roasted quail will be on the menu again tonight." He kissed the top of his fingertips. "Cook always roasts birds which are particularly succulent."

Another laugh got muffled. Juliana liked this side to him. He seemed so relaxed and easy-going. Something felt different between them as if the bonds of master and servant was severed during their competition. *Do not be silly, the earl is not my friend*! She knew many lords were more comfortable around their manservants, who were their constant companions through their daily lives, than with their own families and friends. The bond of trust between master and man grew from mutually knowing their strengths and vulnerabilities.

The bond wasn't one of friendship, and she didn't dare delude herself that more was forming. Not when he made her heart race so, not when she caught herself more than once thinking of what it would be like to dance with him, to be wooed by him. What if she had met him during a fancy ball in town? Would she have captured his regard?

They walked their horses through the forest toward the church, and she did not question why they strolled instead of rode. It felt... peaceful. A dart of a shadow behind some bushes made her falter, and she glanced at the earl to gauge his awareness.

A coiled readiness seemed infused in every line of his body. At this moment, she saw nothing of the easy-going or scholarly gentleman.

"Come out," he said, harshly authoritative.

The bushes rustled, and a boy of about fifteen years emerged, and in his hands were three dead wild birds. He appeared so frightened, Juliana's heart jolted.

"Who are you, boy?"

The earl's voice hadn't softened, and the tension inside her mounted.

"My...my name is Billy, milord," he said in a voice that trembled.

Juliana suddenly understood the boy's fear. This was the earl's land.

"How old are you, boy?" the earl asked, his expression bland.

"Sev...seventeen, milord!"

Her heart ached with sympathy for the boy. Hunting on someone else's land was legally regarded as poaching and had harsh penalties such as deportation or hanging.

"And you are hunting on my lands."

The boy looked at the pheasants in his hand, his face crumpling. "Me sisters and mamma…they be hungry, milord."

Juliana's grip tightened on the rifle. The desperation of the boy had an ache rising in her throat. There were so many pheasants, quails, and woodstock in the massive woods of the earl's estate. Surely a few birds need not be reported. The boy's clothes and boots were threadbare with holes in them, and the thin jacket he wore was bare protection against the cold.

"My lord—" Juliana began, only to stop when he held up a hand.

"You are trying to provide for them?"

"Yes, milord."

"My game warden is Mr. Colby. You'll let him know that you have my permission to hunt these lands whenever in need."

Shock slackened the boy's jaw before his eyes burned bright with hope. "Milord?"

"And you can have these," Juliana said, shrugging from her shoulder the burlap back with their catch of the day. "Perhaps you have neighbors who might also be in need?"

The boy nodded eagerly. "I do, sir." He hurried over for the bag, and he kept sending the earl careful stares as if he were in disbelief of his fortune.

"You might also hunt some more today," the earl offered. "I assume your family is large?"

"Four sisters, my lord, and me mama."

"It is honorable that you take care of them even with such risky ventures. You seem very able with that slingshot.

To have brought down three pheasants with it is no easy feat. Mr. Colby has been looking for a lad of your skills to assist him with his duties. Tell him I recommend your services, and you are to be hired."

The boy scrubbed a hand over his face, and when he spoke, his voice was thick. "Yer lordship...I...do not know what to say."

"Nothing is needed."

The boy bobbed. "I'll hurry to tell me ma the news, your lordship." Then he ran through the woods with nimble speed.

The earl turned to her. "The sky is looking angry, let's —" He faltered and arched a brow. "Why are you smiling at me so? And why in God's name are there tears in your eyes?"

"You were wonderful," she said huskily.

"It was a simple matter, not deserving of such attentions."

"You are wrong, my lord," she said with quiet earnestness. "Since living in England, I have read in the newspapers of boys as young as twelve being hanged for stealing food or game on private lands. He believed you would have him arrested, but instead, you offered him hope and a chance at a future. I...you were kind, thoughtful, and honorable in a situation where many others before you have acted with anger, and rank disregard for the sufferings of others."

He stared at her as if he didn't know what exactly to make of her.

"I—"

Whatever the earl was about to say was lost in a sharp crack of thunder, and the sky opened.

"Your prediction of an hour is woefully wrong," she cried, immediately shivering under the icy droplets.

The earl hurried over, grabbed her by the waist, and helped her atop the horse.

"There is a recently vacant groundsman's cottage nearby, we'll take shelter there," he said, releasing her and rushing to his horse.

Once he mounted, she urged her horse in the direction the earl went. The strength of the rain was shocking, but not entirely unexpected for late October weather.

They cantered through the woods at a brisk pace in the driving icy rain, allowing the horses to pick their way to shelter. Neither beast nor human wanted to be out in this weather any longer than necessary. The scents of damp horses, wet leaves, and the old mulch of the forest permeated her nostrils, exhilarating her. It made her aware of how good it was to be alive and to feel with all her senses. Only the crack of lightning and the regular beat of the horses' hooves broke the surrounding silence. The denizens of the wood, animal and fowl, had sought shelter from the powerful storm.

The rain lashed through her clothes, soaking her hair and running inside her garments to chill and trickle down her skin. Juliana had no thoughts of discovery, only an enjoyment of the freedom of nature around her and her lord's company. Even the discomfort from the cold, drenching rain could not dent her happiness. The ride seemed unending but only took a few minutes, for time had stopped for Juliana.

They passed a final cluster of trees, and a clearing became visible through the darkening deluge of rain. In its center stood a picturesque cottage. The thatched roof patterned with care and pride by a true craftsman. The walls whitewashed and part-timbered in blackened oak. A garden surrounded the cottage and had a mostly barren vegetable patch to one side. Although few flowers bloomed, she imagined in spring and summer it would be a delight. There would be climbing roses creating a bright splash of many-colors that would only add to the beauty of the scene.

It was breathtaking, even suffering the vagaries of the weather with such an intense thunderstorm. The perfumes of wet mint and other herbs drifted on the air while the earl headed to a newer structure behind the cottage. A small barn or stable had been built behind the cottage, and he rode to offer shelter to their steeds first. The earl jumped down, pushing the large doors open to allow the horses room to enter. Juliana followed her master, leading her soaked bay gelding behind the black stallion the earl had ridden.

Inside, the earl had already lit a lamp and was now unsaddling his horse. Juliana did the same with her own mount. She rubbed him down with some clean straw, for she could not spot brushes or combs to groom him properly. There were three stalls, so she led the horse to one and then looked around for feed or hay. She noticed some hay, although it was not of the best quality, the horse seemed prepared to eat it, given there was nothing better. The earl had dealt with his steed in a like manner, and then he headed from the outhouse with two empty buckets.

Juliana watched as he scooped water from a horse trough she had not noticed before. He carried the water to each horse, shutting the stall gates behind them. He then picked up the lit lamp and headed back to the doors, with Juliana following.

The earl secured the doors behind them with a simple large bolt and led the way to the cottage. He located a key that was uninventively hidden beneath a large plant pot. It turned easily in the lock and allowed them to enter. The oil lamp's light showed a moderately sized room with a closed range, rustic wooden table, chairs pleasantly cushioned, and a large fireplace. The fire was already arranged and ready to light, and there was a pile of cut dry firewood neatly stacked beside it.

Juliana helped the earl from his greatcoat and hung it from pegs on the back of the front door. She shucked out of her own coat and put it on another hook, leaving both their hats and riding gloves on a chair beside the door, to drip gently until they could be moved closer to the fire to dry.

She noticed the earl had placed his Manton beside the chair and moved hers beside it. The earl was lighting the fire, so she checked the range, finding it also ready for lighting. She found a tinderbox, and carefully using a spill of wood, lit the kindling. It sparked immediately, and she blew on the flame to make sure the fire took. It was soon burning brightly, and she shut the stove's door and left it to warm.

Juliana noticed a door to the right of the stove and opened it. It revealed a small room almost filled by a large bed already made up with a patchwork quilt, sheets, and pillows. It was very inviting. The earl naked within those sheets, staring into her eyes and stroking her hair, flashed through her mind. She reddened, realizing her vision had not provided a nightdress for herself, and that she had been as naked as her employer.

Then as the fire the earl had lit blazed to life, he stripped off his sodden clothes, draping them precisely over a wooden chair to dry in front of the fire. Juliana gulped and smothered a gasp as he removed his jacket, waistcoat, and shirt. He sat and pulled off his own boots and wet stockings, then undid the fall at the front of his breeches.

Dear heavens, he plans to get naked!

"My lord," she squeaked, then slapped a hand over her mouth. Had he heard the slip in her tone? She hoped the sleeting rain had covered her cry.

He glanced over at Juliana. "Come on, get out of those wet things and get dried, or you will catch your death of cold," he said, staring at her with a glint in his eyes, daring her to follow through.

"No, I will be fine, I think we should return to the main house. I am tougher than I look and will survive a little rain…" she said, but her cheeks were heating, and she could see amusement in the earl's eyes.

His hands went to the front of his riding breeches.

"Your Lordship, do not remove those breeches!"

He froze, his gaze gleaming. "Why not?"

"There is a rat, my lord." She made a measurement with her hands. "He was behind you just now."

The earl grinned. "And he was that big, hmm?"

"*Yes*, and surely should you remove your breeches, he… well, he might attack your backside."

For a moment, the earl just stared at her, then his shoulders shook with laughter, which rolled from him rich and warm. The sound of it did fluttery things to her heart.

Lips still quirking, he asked, "Tell me, my good lad, have you ever been naked before a man or a woman?"

She gasped. "I…my lord! It is not fitting to ask me that!"

He took a few steps toward her. "And why is that so?"

"I…no, I am…you are being a right rogue!"

Provoking amusement lit in his eyes. "I've never been accused of *that* before, and most certainly did not expect it from a fellow man. How intriguingly novel."

There was a question in his voice, a challenge, but Juliana was unsure how to respond.

"You will catch a cold if you do not remove more of those sodden clothes. At least remove your waistcoat, jacket, and stockings. As men together…it is entirely proper for us to remain in our trousers."

Her heart pounding a fierce beat, she stared at him mutely, sodden, and frankly miserable.

"I cannot," she whispered, an intolerable ache in her throat.

This time his smile was gentle, almost understanding. Yet, she detected tension in his frame. "I suppose I had better redress then and ride back to the house to have a carriage fetched for you?"

"In this storm?"

"Yes. I cannot have you fall ill."

She could tell that he was most sincere in that regard, and this went far beyond him rattling her composure.

He retrieved his wet clothes and put them back on.

And she could only stand there, staring at him, wondering if she should just blurt out the truth.

He is kind and thoughtful. Perhaps he might listen to her plight, maybe he might forgive her deception.

Or perhaps he'll have me arrested!

CHAPTER 8

Wentworth was losing perspective. Now was not the time to be thinking about how pretty and desirable Julian appeared. Not when they were alone in a secluded cottage with little to no chance of discovery. The possibilities for debauchery were wicked, scandalous, and endless.

He was not a bloody rogue who would take advantage of a lady's heated and unquestionably aroused state. Wentworth felt shaken on a level he'd never experienced before. "I must leave," he said. "I'll be back."

A gusty sigh of relief left Julian, and she moved toward the rifles in the corner of the door. "I'll come with you."

"No!"

Julian's eyes widened at his vehemence, and a frown creased her forehead.

"It is raining fiercely. To be out in this deluge, you might catch your death of cold. I'll come back for you with an umbrella or send a footman."

"If it is not wise for me to be out in the rain, my lord, it cannot be safe for you either!"

"I believe my constitution is sturdier. A stiff wind would blow you over," he muttered crossly.

He made to walk away, and a hand grabbed him, the force enough to make him turn around.

"You are leaving without your coat and hat!"

"Hang the coat and hat," he growled.

Julian looked a little anxiously at him. "Do not dare leave me in this creepy cottage alone!"

"By God, are you afraid of the damn rain?"

"No…just a bit of the thunder, and you must admit the sky has darkened rather ominously. We are surrounded by miles of woods, and those branches are swaying rather furiously in the wind. And look at the brambles scraping the windows. They are like long gnarled fingers belonging to something…I don't know, ghost-like."

"You are entirely serious," Wentworth said, considerably astonished.

At least Julian had the grace to look sheepish.

"You are a grown man." *Woman…you are a woman, and I can tell because of how you are staring at me. With such heat and want…yet, you are also skittish.* "I must leave," he said tightly.

"Stay with me," she whispered, those lovely lavender eyes rounded and imploring.

"No."

Now a scowl settled on her face. "Why not?"

"Because…" Wentworth swallowed, or tried to past the lump of raw need rising in his throat.

"Because?"

"Because of *this*." And he hauled her against his body and took her mouth in a burning kiss.

His valet gripped his jacket and froze. Not even her chest moved; it was as if she ceased breathing. Wentworth opened his eyes to find hers also open and wide like saucers. He held her gaze, their mouths still pressed together, both so still it was a miracle they were able to maintain the position.

He had always asked permission before kissing a lady. Even with his lovers, there had always been an indication he was about to touch or kiss them, as it was a step a gentleman should follow. He was a gentleman; he always thought of a lady's sensibility as a gentleman should. Except, staring at Julian stirred a passion that felt raw and primitive. Wentworth didn't want to ask any permission. He wanted to take, wanted to ravish.

"My...My lord," she said achingly soft. "I…"

"I know...I *know* you are a lady."

Breathing was nearly impossible as he waited for her to move, to say something, to deny it, to run from him, to even scream. Anything but this silence. At her shocked, prolonged lack of response, Wentworth spoke. "I just might prove the theory of dying from an internal heat generated by an unexplained force—spontaneous combustion, as proposed by Giuseppe Bianchini. However, the force in my case is not mysterious; it is *you*. By God, I feel if I do not kiss you...taste you even once, I will expire on the fucking spot."

Her face flushed a delicate rosy hue at his crudeness, but the delight that entered her eyes sparked his desire like a match to dry kindling.

"You know?"

How husky and soft her voice was.

"Yes."

"You cannot be sure."

"I am most certain."

"How—"

"I can feel it in the ache of want I have for you."

She stared at him for a few moments, and then rather doubtfully asked, "And you are not angry?"

"I *am* curious…intrigued."

Her breath puffed across his lips as she murmured, "An odd reaction to deception. Most would send for the magistrate."

"I am the kind of gentleman who prefers to see ingenuity, inventiveness, and practicality in life choices that assume many risks. The foundation of any discovery first relies on the risk one is willing to take to prove themselves."

Tender humor lit in her eyes, and he felt the curve of her mouth against his. "You, my lord, are entirely kissable."

With a groan of defeat, he took her mouth with his. And to his eternal relief, she flung her hands around his neck, stretched up onto her toes, and returned his kiss with artless but such passionate ardor.

Thank Christ.

Her mouth tasted incredibly sweet. Her responses wonderfully wanton. Wentworth gathered her closer in his embrace and kissed her with more intimacy. She gasped against his mouth, and he kissed her more carnally, sliding his tongue against hers.

She made a wanton, achy sound that went right to his

cock. Bloody hell. His manhood rose, a pulse-pounding need throbbing through him. Their lips parted briefly, and their gazes collided. In her, there was an answering arousal that had the headiest effect on his senses.

"What is your proper name?" he asked, clearing the roughness of desire from his throat.

"Juliana. My…my father and my brother often call me Jules."

Now he understood why she chose Julian as her incognito name.

He reached out and pulled the wig from her head to reveal tightly pinned dark tresses. Wentworth removed six pins, dropping them to the floor. She lifted her hand and did the rest until her hair fanned out across her shoulders and down her chest.

"Your hair is beautiful."

"I had to cut it…before it was waist length."

He touched the silken strands. Her beauty was drawn into sharper relief, all that mass of black hair, a slightly tanned skin, and exquisite lavender eyes. Had her skin always looked so soft and flushed? So inviting? He wanted to kiss all over her body and imprint the feel and taste of her in his mind.

"You are so lovely," he said gruffly, dipping to catch her mouth in a brief kiss.

When he made to pull back, she followed, wrapping her hands firmly around his neck.

"Jump up," he muttered against her mouth.

And she did, with no hesitation. This brought their mouths more in line with each other, but it also did something far more dangerous. To hold her to him and support her slight weight, Wentworth gripped her lush backside with his hands, and she hooked her ankles behind his back.

His cock, which was stiff and aching, was flushed to her heated center.

They both stilled under the realization of just how intimate they were. But he saw no anxiety or fear in her eyes, only need and curiosity.

"Have you had a lover before?" he asked with a measure of desperation, wishing she had experience.

"You were my very first kiss," she said a bit shyly.

Ah, hell. She was just as sweetly innocent as he suspected. Wentworth couldn't take advantage. That would make him a right bounder, a rogue with no redeemable gentlemanly qualities. "I...bloody hell...this is dangerous, we must stop at once and—"

Juliana caught his words with her mouth, swallowing his muffled groan of surprise and delight.

❦

Juliana never imagined a kiss could be this pleasing...this decadent. The earl tasted heady and something sweetly elusive. The place between her legs ached something fierce, and the warnings from her mother about cads and rakes clanged a distant alarm in her passion hazed thoughts.

He's no rake, she thought, kissing him with such fervor, *just a gentleman who desires me.*

The earl walked with her draped around his waist. She whimpered into the kiss as the movement had her female sex brushing against something hard and throbbing, causing somewhere deep inside her belly to quicken, sending powerful darts of longing through her.

Her back was pressed against the walls for the room, and he did something with his hips, a push, or a swivel. Good heavens! Shocked by the sensation that shot through her belly, she trembled in his embrace.

He broke their kiss, and his lips glistened with wetness, and his face was harsh with restrained desire. His eyes searched her face, and she blushed at her very unrestrained responses.

"We need to get you out of these clothes. You are cold and shivering."

He stepped back and eased her down. Juliana did not speak but removed her neck cloth and waistcoat, then drew the soaked shirt over her head. Beneath all of that was a linen binding that was also wet.

She glanced up. "I'll not remove this."

He walked over to the bed and tugged off the small coverlet. "You must. You are still trembling."

Juliana was, but she didn't know if it was from her wet garments or the introduction to pleasure. With his back turned to her, he said, "Remove it all and then use this to wrap yourself. I'll not look."

"Thank you, my lord."

"Wentworth," he said softly. "Please, Juliana, call me Wentworth."

She smiled, and trusting him, quickly removed the bindings which had made her already small breasts nonexistent. Recalling how buxom his mistress had been, she wondered what the earl with such experience would think of her petite shape. Annoyed, she pushed aside those thoughts and removed her trousers and undergarment.

Juliana took the sheet and wrapped it around her three times before tying the front in the style of a toga.

"You may turn around my…Wentworth."

He faced her, and she stared at him, terribly aware she was absolutely naked beneath the sheets.

"You are blushing," he said with a measure of amusement. "I still cannot believe I thought you could be a lad."

She smiled. "I had a very good disguise."

He took her clothes and wig to the fire so they might dry.

He waved toward the small table and the two chairs by the small window. "Will you sit with me?"

Juliana made her way over and lowered herself into the surprisingly comfortable chair. The earl sat before her, and when he reached over and took her hands within his, a sigh left her, and her shoulders relaxed.

"I do not know why you are hiding, but if you wish to tell me, I will do all that I can to assist you."

She cleared her throat. "My brother, Mr. Robert Pryce. He gave me your name as a gentleman I could turn to should I find myself in a difficult position."

The earl frowned, and she saw no recognition in his eyes.

"You do not recall my brother."

He smiled sheepishly. "We must have met, more than once, too, for him to have recommended me."

"But you perhaps looked right through him," she murmured, thinking of how her brother had spoken of the earl's brilliance with such admiration. "However, I do not think Robert imagined I might have ever needed help of such magnitude."

"And where is your brother?"

"He is on his way to London from New York. Based on his last letter, he should be here before Christmas."

"And what did you want from me?"

She hesitated. "A place to stay away from society until my birthday in six weeks' time. I visited your townhouse, but it was at a time of upheaval. You were withdrawing to the country, your valet had left to be with his ailing mother, and your household needed a replacement. They also gave me the impression you would not be distracted from your current mathematical problem to meet with me. My situation was desperate…"

"And your ingenuity rose inside to save you."

She smiled. "If you wish to see it in such a manner, I have no objection."

"What made your situation desperate?"

Juliana withdrew her hands from his to lean back in her chair. "A scoundrel was trying to force me into a marriage. The morning I arrived at your townhouse, I had escaped a kidnapping."

"By God!" Wentworth frowned and folded his arms across his chest. "Which bounder did this."

"Mr. Matthew Chevers."

The earl's lips curled with disdain. "He is known to me. I had not thought him so dishonorable."

"I never suspected his character to be so wormy either."

Shrewdness glinted in the earl's eyes. "Why did he try to force you? Are you wealthy?"

"Very."

One of his brows winged upward.

"Once my brother reaches me and I am five and twenty, no one will be able to force me into any marriage."

A shudder of distaste went through her, and the earl's eyes sharpened.

"Do you never want to marry? Or is it only this despicable ass you have such an aversion toward?"

How curious he hadn't asked of her worth. Almost everyone who realized she was an heiress found a way to ask how much money she had, even though they pretended to believe it crass to speak so openly of money.

"I do not wish to marry."

He stilled, and curiously, an unfathomable expression settled on his face. "Ever?"

She grinned. "Is that so weird to believe, my lord? I overheard your mother lamenting this morning, your failure on the marriage mart. I believe once again; we have something in common."

He glanced away from her for a moment, a small smile about his lips.

"I simply hadn't found a lady I like. It is not a deep aversion."

"You were looking?" she asked, considerably astonished.

"No," he said, humor lighting in his eyes. "I'd planned to do so when I reached five and thirty. That is a good seven years from now. Why do you never wish to marry? I thought this was a dream of most young ladies."

She rolled her eyes, stood, and walked over to the small window, staring out into the sleeting rain. She felt his presence at her back and acting on the impulse; she leaned against his hardened frame.

Juliana closed her eyes, a feeling of contentment sweeping through her when he slipped his arms around her. Being in this small cottage felt like they had shut out the outside world, and it was wonderful.

"My inheritance is left to me by my father, who worked to leave his children legacies. I will not marry a fortune hunter so he might squander my father's hard work in a few months."

"Not all gentlemen are fortune hunters."

"I know," she said with a sigh. "I was but thinking about the gentlemen who courted me over these last few seasons."

She felt the jolt of his heart.

"You were out about during the season?"

"Yes. Viscount Bramley is my stepfather."

"I did not notice you," he said gruffly.

"I am not that memorable."

"Rubbish. No one could dare forget your eyes or your voice. I know I will never be able to scrub them from my memories. And certainly not the taste of you."

Juliana turned in the cage of his arms and peered up at him. "You flatter me, my lord," she whispered, bestowing a warm smile upon him.

"I only spoke the truth."

"My father had many dreams, but he died before he could fulfill all of them. One was to open a grand shop, an emporium with different departments tailored to the middle class. Also, a hospital, he wanted to build a hospital. I mean to see some of his dreams realized."

"Here, in London?"

"In New York."

He stilled. "You plan to return home?"

"Oh, yes! I have wanted to return for a couple years. It is the best way to honor him, and the best use of the wealth he left me." Juliana wrinkled her nose. "Could you believe Mr. Chevers spoke of the barouche he would buy once he controlled my inheritance? That was the limits to his imaginings, a damn coach!"

Wentworth tucked a wisp of hair behind her ear. "Your dreams are good ones, do not let them go. Certainly not for something so ordinary as marriage."

Her heart warmed. "Perhaps in a few years, once I've accomplished some of my plans, I'll marry a gentleman who has a genuine affection for me in his heart and will not mind his wife is a businesswoman."

"A businesswoman," he murmured, "a truly scandalous proposition."

Juliana laughed. "I do not dare think my husband could be a man from the *Bon Ton*. My pursuits would only make his life within his society awkward; wouldn't you agree?"

"If he wants you, none of that will matter."

The way he stared at her…Juliana's heart ached, and she wished she understood the expression in his eyes.

So how did she go on now? There were still six weeks before her five and twentieth birthday, and she needed to lie low in disguise to prevent discovery by her stepfather and his son. She would be prey to other men if she tried to find lodgings or work somewhere else. But was she not more at risk when the earl clearly wanted to seduce her?

Who would have ever imagined he could be such a rake?

Juliana had feared that if he realized exactly who she was and the size of her fortune, he might offer marriage for the same reasons as Matthew. But he was so different. "What happens once we leave the cottage?" she whispered.

"You'll continue with your ruse until your birthday."

Her eyes widened. This she had not expected. He was a man she found intriguing, good company, and incredibly attractive. Could she really stay for the next six weeks in his home…still as his valet, knowing how weak she was to his touches, to his kisses?

"Why? Wouldn't it be better for me to reappear as a guest in your home, Miss Juliana Pryce? Your mother and aunt are underfoot, so it will be very proper should anyone raise a fuss."

"Juliana…"

"Yes."

"Everyone who has seen or interacted with you at Norbrook Park will know that Miss Juliana Pryce and my valet Julian are the same."

She laughed. "Rubbish!"

He sent her a glance of considerable surprise. "Surely you jest?"

"I do not."

"Juliana…" he scrubbed a hand over his face. "You are a beautiful flame; only a fool would not recognize. My mother, who only saw you briefly, will most certainly not miss it or the other servants you've been around for several days. I've never seen eyes the color of lavender before, nor such delicate slanted cheekbones. You…those features will be unmissable because you are so very remarkable."

A tender feeling welled inside her, and she felt warm all over. "Beautiful, hmm?"

He lowered his head. "And I also do not think as Miss Pryce I will be able to do this…"

He kissed her, slanting his mouth over hers with ravishing greed. And with a moan, she helplessly responded. Juliana's heart sang with an odd happiness.

"But as my valet," he said hotly against her mouth. "Ah, Juliana, should you desire it, the possibilities are so very naughty *and* endless."

Good heavens, why was she so tempted?

CHAPTER 9

A fter tempting Julianna with that very wicked glint in his eyes, the earl moved away to open the door and peered outside. The storm had lifted, leaving a sullen sky with the sun attempting to fight its way through still gray clouds.

"We should dress and return to our proper places, with my mother and family in occupation our prolonged absence will be noticed, though I would much prefer to stay here longer and get to know you much better," he said.

"Yes, of course, my lord," Juliana said, checking that their clothes had mostly dried in front of the fire.

"Wentworth…whenever we are alone."

She smiled but offered no reply. Juliana got redressed, a bit mortified to look directly at him, recalling how hot and wanton she'd been returning his kisses. She allowed the earl such liberties with her person and had enjoyed every kiss of their delightful interlude.

Pushing aside such thoughts, she re-pinned her hair so she could tuck on her wig. Although Wentworth gallantly

turned his back, she tried not to look at his beautiful body
as he donned his clothes but found herself sneaking peeks.
She wanted not to think about him but was unable to
direct her thoughts elsewhere. With a scowl, Juliana
admitted she was unsure how she felt about the earl. He
desired her, and she found him attractive. Perhaps more
than attractive, for Juliana had been overwhelmed by the
contact between their mouths and bodies.

But did she want more beyond that fleeting interlude
of passionate kisses? They had no future together, so why
would more kisses be of any point?

Pleasure, something wayward inside her whispered. *Fun
and pleasure*. Things denied to her even though she did not
believe in the English lofty ideas of propriety. Decorum
was also observed in New York, but certainly not with the
measures of restrictions and hypocrisy she had witnessed
during her London seasons.

They relocked the cottage and saddled their horses,
riding in silence back to the main house. Upon arriving,
they handed their mounts over to a stable lad. The young
boy tugged his forelock in respect to his master. Then, she
and the earl both slipped into the manor by a side door.

"You should probably get smartened up and stay in the
background as much as possible. My aunt and cousins
might not notice you are female, but my mother is very
astute and little gets by her, so try to stay out of her
notice," Wentworth instructed her.

"I should get your own clothes ready first, my lord,"
Juliana said, trying to get back in her role as a valet.

A slight frown creased his brows. "I can dress myself,
Juliana."

She stared up at him, then slowly nodded.

"You can deal with these clothes when you look respectable yourself. Looking crumpled will only draw questioning glances your way."

"I will be careful," she replied and then hurried off to her chamber.

THE FOLLOWING MORNING, Juliana woke later feeling vexed and restless. She was not the kind of person to lust after a gentleman, and certainly not one like the earl. Yet she had dreamed of his warm lips touching, teasing, and tasting hers, driving her wild with passion.

She had been in the earl's home for eleven days and had already kissed him. And was inappropriately dreaming about it…longing for more. Why not enjoy the earl in her bed before she went about her life? She would most likely never see him again. Her plan was to return to New York to be closer to her father's sister, Aunt Felicity, and her daughters, to open up her own business, and to implement all the plans she'd made with her brother over the years.

But I must remain hidden for a few more weeks.

"What if I should permit more than kisses from the earl?" she whispered to the walls. The idea was so deliciously shocking, a pulse of wanton heat throbbed between her folds.

She rolled over in the small bed and pressed her face into the feathered pillows, hoping to cool the heat in her cheeks.

Why not, I am four and twenty! A spinster by society's definition, even in New York.

And when she returned to New York, her energy would be directed to meeting with her lawyers, other business owners, architects as she picked a few of the businesses from her father's dusty portfolio to bring to life. There would be no time for flirting or romantic attachments. Her time here with the earl would be a wonderful memory to treasure for a lifetime.

She pushed from the bed with an irritated murmur and padded over to the sole window in her chamber. Juliana stood for a long time before her room's small window, gazing up at a thoroughly overcast sky.

The only thoughts that should preoccupy her mind were how to deal with her stepfather should he uncover the heiress, Juliana Pryce before her birthday. Though she believed that chance was slim to non-existent, her father had taught her it was best in life to prepare for all eventualities.

Wentworth was a kind and honorable man, and Juliana sensed should she prevail upon him, he would help her in every way possible. She pressed a palm right above the rising ache in her heart. He made her crave things that went against her self-reliant nature.

Juliana really liked and admired his character. In another time and another world, she would have dreamed about the earl courting her.

I know I should not obsess about Wentworth, because he will not fit into my long-term plans. Yet his kisses awakened my body so sweetly that my mind was befuddled by him. My body and mind seem to desire different things, and I am not sure how to deal with that!

Perhaps once settled in New York, she could invite him

to visit her. *And why would he?* A very annoying inner voice asked.

"Because our friendship is…" Well, Juliana wasn't certain they were even friends. A deep restlessness stirred, and an ache for something more rose inside her heart. She pressed her palm against the cold windowpane, at a loss as to why she spent so much time thinking about the dratted earl.

Not because of a kiss!

She blew out a sharp breath, not liking to admit he had dwelled in her thoughts *before* those delightful kisses in the cottage. Juliana had never permitted herself to think of life in London or marrying a gentleman here. She had always known that she would return to New York and assume her role in the family business. Her brother hadn't objected to her plans, for he valued her input greatly, and he solicited her advice often. They currently had a shipping company, a brewery, and a general clothing store that took up several storefronts and rose two stories in New York. They rented out the offices and apartments above the emporium. Her brother admired her dream to expand their father's empire and had tossed his hat and innovative ideas into their planning.

Juliana felt he would be bitterly disappointed if he even knew that she had wavered in her plans, even for a moment.

And I did not, she reminded herself fiercely, *I simply wondered what it would be like to have the earl woo me.*

"But I'll not think of such nonsense," she muttered, "one kiss, and I am thinking of courtship!"

The only thing she needed to concentrate on was her

own safety, maintaining her disguise, and serving the earl without compromising her heart.

As she turned around to dress and prepare for the day, the naughtiest thought invaded her mind, *everything else can be gambled with…*

Conclusion: My valet is unquestionably a woman, who has revealed her reasons for perpetuating such a ruse. She, Juliana, expected me to be angry at her deception, but I was not. I admire a woman of imagination and initiative, and she also strikes me as a highly creative sort.

Now that my brief experiment has come to a far quicker end than I anticipated, I feel a sense of loss. Why, I am not entirely sure. We shared some prolonged and heated kisses in the cottage as we hid from the fierce storm, and I confess when I planned this experiment, I did not predict my own powerful reaction to her accurately.

My attraction has grown considerably, and I must admit I have never felt the emotions brewing inside my heart for another. I wonder if it is not too soon to feel such a profound connection to a lady with such intensity. Then I am reminded of her wit, her bravery, her kindness, and the lush, sweet taste of her mouth.

Intriguingly, she is not interested in marriage. I had thought it an obvious solution, but she dismissed that suggestion out of hand. I was rather taken aback by her vehemence and found her independence refreshing and somewhat lowering to find my own person so easily rejected. Although I admire her drive to be a businesswoman, even if it removes her from being a candidate to be my countess. Even more fascinating is how my heart pounds upon writing that she might be lost to me as a wife. I find that I am also the subject of my own experiment!

I was not clear in expressing my own interest in her and did not directly propose or indicate that my feelings might be engaged. Do I want to consider Miss Juliana Pryce as a lady to woo: A resounding yes!

I believe wholeheartedly in respecting her decisions for her dreams and future. Yet I've never wanted another as I want her. I can easily tell it goes beyond simple physical attraction.

Is the course of action to take, am I considering seducing an innocent lady of quality, persuading her into being my lover? That would make me a right rogue…

"Excuse me, my lord. But the ladies are insisting you take tea with them in the green salon and say that if you do not attend, they will drag you from your work, sir," his butler informed him.

"I will come at once, thank you, Bernard."

Wentworth paused in his writing, blotting the ink and sliding his journal into a drawer and locking it. His family could be far too inquisitive. He strolled to the room they had directed him to and sat in the armchair closest to the windows. His mother, aunt, and two cousins started talking, but he still considered the quandary that Juliana's presence in his home and heart created.

"Wentworth, are you at all present?" the strident demand of his aunt's voice pulled him back to the present.

He settled his gaze on her, a bit amused at the narrow eyed glare she directed at him. His aunt was still a fine-looking woman, her posture militarily precise and formidable. Her vibrant, auburn hair was ruthlessly coaxed into a stylish chignon with only a few luxuriant curls allowed to break its silhouette. She had never been a great beauty, but her strong bone structure had survived aging better than many of the delicate diamonds of society with whom she had competed to make an eligible marriage in her youth.

Her dress was plain in a beautiful green material, ornamented only by a deep lace collar and cuffs. Against the pastel greens of the room's décor, it showed her to advantage. Wentworth acknowledged that her taste was excellent and that she knew it suited her still trim figure.

Slowly, he closed the leather-bound book he had taken with him and rested it on the small table between the sofas. "Of course, Aunt Millicent, forgive my distraction, my attention is now wholly yours."

She arched a brow at that, smiling.

What had they been discussing? Ah yes, the ball and who to invite.

"I will happily consent if it is to be a masquerade ball," Wentworth said smoothly, lowering the book. "Is that possible?"

Henrietta gasped and clapped her hands. "A wonderful idea, we've never held a masked ball before," she cried, sharing a swift glance of mischief with her sister, who had been idly running her hands over the pianoforte. She wore a gown of delicate pinks marred, in his opinion, by a profusion of flounces and bows, which distracted from her dainty beauty.

"And you'll not attend this one either," Wentworth replied, accepting the cup of tea his mother handed to him. "Thank you, Mother."

The twins' expressions became crestfallen.

"Mamma!" Isabelle cried, "Please say it isn't so! We'll be here where it is most safe. Please say Henrietta and I may attend."

Aunt Millicent arched a brow. "Why a masked ball, Wentworth? It seems so unlike you! You usually grumble about hosting any event at Norbrook Park."

"Yet you do so every year, and I do not intend to be doing any of the work to arrange it, Aunt," he said indulgently.

Aunt Millicent paused, giving her head a tiny shake.

"Who cares?" his mother asked, delicately dabbing her mouth with her serviette. "I *am* astonished my son has agreed, and I'm exceedingly glad. We are to have a ball! We should get to planning it right away. Say two or three weeks?"

"Yes," Aunt Millicent said. "And your dear cousin is in the right, my girls, a masked ball is not for you. That will make it much harder to chaperone your willful ways."

The girls vehemently protested, but their mother shooed them out, following closely behind. Their arguments slowly faded away, and he bit back his smile of amusement. "They are a handful."

"They are," his mother said with a gusty smile. "And at times like these, I am most thankful you were my only darling child."

Wentworth chuckled and took a sip of his tea.

"I am surprised you did not protest about this ball," she said softly, peering at him as if she was trying to read his thoughts. "But thank you. I am happy to arrange it with Millicent's able assistance. I'll invite the squire's daughter, Miss Lavinia, she has shown considerable interest in you and is the *loveliest* girl. And Viscount Sheffield's eldest daughter is in the parish visiting an aunt. Do you recall the eldest of Sheffield's daughters?"

Wentworth lowered his cup, wishing he had something more robust. His mother had that glint in her eyes, warning him she was just getting warmed to her topic. However, instead of brushing it aside as he'd always done, he considered her. "Mother?"

"Yes, my dear?"

"Why is it so important for you that I marry?"

Her eyes widened, and she lowered the pastry back to the small plate. "You never asked me that before."

"I know."

She smiled, but he spied a sadness behind it, which jolted his heart. "Mother?"

"I suppose I wish to see you happy. A companion to keep you company, someone to help you find pleasures in life."

His darling mother blushed, and he almost choked upon realizing the pleasures she possibly referred to. "Do you not think since I will be the one spending the rest of my days with this prospective lady, I should be the one to look for her?"

She sent him a cross glare. "Absolutely not. If I should wait on you to be torn away from your books, I'll be an old, lonely woman with no grandchildren to dote on with one foot in the grave and the other somewhere else."

Loneliness. It struck him then that had been the emotion that had pierced her eyes earlier. Since his father's death some eight years' prior, his mother spent a great deal of time with her sister. He glanced around the private drawing-room, wondering at the memories it roused for her. She and his father had often been in this very room, laughing and playing whist together, and then kissing like they were young lovers.

The memory warmed Wentworth. "You miss father?"

"Every day." She cast him a birdlike look of inquiry. "Do you?"

He jerked. "Mother?"

"I only asked because you rarely speak of him."

Wentworth drew in a deep, steady breath. "I might not think of him every day or speak of him often, but he is in my heart, mother, and he lingers in the shadows of everything I do. When I am working on an equation, and it frustrates me, I can hear his voice in my head, a calm and encouraging force that has never failed me."

How was he just realizing with his father gone, and Wentworth a grown man she could no longer fuss over, his mother desired someone to dote on—grandchildren. Now he understood why she spent so much time with Aunt Millicent and the girls. "And who are these ladies you think will make me a suitable match?"

His mother's face brightened as if he'd handed her the keys to a kingdom.

"Oh, Wentworth," she cried, clapping her hands together. "At first, I thought someone the opposite of your reserved nature would be perfect. And I thought Miss Mary, Lord Barton's daughter, would be that person. She is incredibly beautiful, but not too bright. Miss Mary is also overly concerned with fashion and who's who in society. I think you would tire of that soon. Miss Sheffield is a bit of a bluestocking, very bookish, and even formed a literary saloon right in her father's home. She is a lovely girl, but I am not sure of the advantage of putting two people together who lose themselves in books and academic pursuits."

"Is that not the same as putting two people together who enjoy attending balls and social events? They will merely have pursuits in common, which is a good thing for any marriage, I might imagine."

His mother smiled widely. "Wonderful, so I might rely on you to ask Miss Sheffield for a dance at the ball. Perhaps two. I will invite her to stay with us for a few days. You could be very discreet but take long walks with her, go riding around the lanes, see if you like her."

Something in him recoiled at that notion, and his heart lurched. Wentworth took the time to recall the ladies his mother spoke about. "I've met these ladies?"

"You have, and this season you partnered Miss Mary in a quadrille and even a waltz. You made such a charming pair."

"Mother," Wentworth began thoughtfully, "I doubt I made an impression on these ladies."

"Oh, pish, you are very charming when—"

"And mother, I do not recall these ladies, though I am sure they were lovely with fine qualities. But they are not the sort of ladies I would look to court. I will be fine in selecting the lady I want to be my wife," he said, "with no interference from you, mother."

Wentworth liked his ladies to have spunk, daring, charming wit, and if he wooed a lady, it would be a woman like Miss Juliana Pryce. But what traits should his wife have? Should they share similar interests, or be opposites, or should their compatibility be based purely on the heart? With every passing hour, the liking he felt for Juliana intensified, and she wasn't even in the same room. To be wholly consumed by one's wife must be a boon for matrimony.

"Of course, I would heartily approve whoever you select after whatever experiment you conduct," his mother said with a cheeky smile. "Why do you appear so astonished? Do you not recall that even as a child to select the dishes you wished to eat, you wanted to run an experiment?"

Wentworth laughed, a surge of love for her going through his heart. He recalled how much she had indulged his whims and eccentricities. How proud she'd been of him when he'd been granted early admission into University.

"I have a most marvelous notion," the countess said, coming to her feet. "I will send a letter to Miss Sheffield and ask her to visit. Perhaps once you see Miss Sheffield, you might remember her and that you had liked her."

Wentworth stood and firmly said, "Mother, no. I will not hesitate to boot her from my home, and I daresay my rudeness might be considered another eccentricity."

She scowled. "I—"

At her sharp inhalation, he went over to her, gently clasping her shoulders. "What is it?"

"You…you have someone in your heart," she said, her eyes misting. "I can see it now. My dear son!"

Wentworth stiffened and lowered his arm. "There is someone."

"Oh, why didn't you say so! Who is she?"

Tugging at his necktie, he said, "I do have a strong liking for this young lady, but I am not entirely certain what to do with these feelings. I am not even certain I wish to pursue her."

"We are at feelings?" She demanded with a wide smile. "Let me invite—"

"Mother," he said gently. "Leave it alone. This is my matter, and if something should ever come out of our friendship, you will be the first to know."

She beamed at him.

A glance through the windows showed the very woman he spoke about, dressed as his manservant trudging out of the woodlands bordering the estate. She had been gone now for half of the day. Upon waking this morning, his morning toiletries had been neatly laid out, and he'd dressed alone. She had been there behind his chair in the dining room for breakfast, waiting to serve his every need. He'd spent the morning in his study, going over the books from his steward and the reports on a few investments that had been highly profitable this year.

He hadn't rung for her, suspecting she needed the space to think...to breathe, and he also felt a measure of unease commanding an obvious young lady of quality to serve him. Wentworth dipped and pressed a kiss to the countess's cheek. "If you will excuse me, mother, I will see you at dinner."

He made his way toward the door, intending to stroll outside and meet Juliana.

"Wentworth?"

He stopped and turned to his mother.

She wore an expression of deep curiosity. "Are you still

lost in your mind…I mean…your books?" His mother huffed gently. "What I mean to ask is, this young lady who has caught your interest, is she or thoughts of her able to pull you away from your books?"

He knew why his mother asked. Wentworth had skillfully avoided the entanglement of eligible young ladies these past few years because he was more interested in his books. Always. "What books?" he asked.

Her eyes widened, and a delighted laugh slipped from her. He bowed and exited the room smiling.

CHAPTER 10

I t didn't take long for Wentworth to cut across the
rolling lawns of his estate to where he'd seen Juliana
through the windows. There was a nip in the air, and in the
distance, the dogs raced across the grounds, playing.
Wentworth veered onto a beaten track, which led to the
lake on the property's eastern side. He spied her lying on
the grassy banking, elbows draped across her forehead and
her eyes closed. Now he saw her as a woman. Even dressed
in male clothes, he realized what an attractive picture she
made in repose. His breath hitched slightly, and he felt a
strange sense of possession and longing that she would
come to feel something deeper than attraction and
gratitude to him.

The backdrop of the wintry lake with swans gliding on
the slightly rippling water presented a pleasing vista. The
stark skeletons of the now naked trees reflected in the
water, and the blue sky decorated by a few small fluffy
clouds only added to the scene's tranquility, and he felt

happy. He briefly examined the emotion but accepted that Juliana being there was the main reason for that sensation.

Careful not to jolt her, he made his way over and lowered himself to the grass. He, too, watched the sky, waiting for her to stir. She was aware of his presence, for he could see the wild fluttering of her pulse at the base of her throat where she'd untied her neck cloth.

He sprawled on the grass beside her, staring up at the sky.

"I went for a jaunt in the village," she offered. "I cut across the woods of your estate."

"I noticed. Was it pleasant?"

The grass crinkled as she rustled. "At first. Then I realized just how far I had to walk."

He chuckled at the wry humor in her tone. "You may take the carriage even to do personal errands."

"Thank you."

They fell into a comfortable silence, and he was contented with watching the puffy clouds gently sweep across the sky while he mentally calculated the probability of rain. In the distance, the bright colors of a rainbow painted the sky with its beautiful colors. "Juliana, do you know how rainbows are formed?"

"Yes."

He turned his head on the grass and stared at her.

Humor danced in her beautiful eyes. "After Our Lord washed away the evil in Noah's time, he promised never to destroy immorality with a flood again. So, whenever there is rain, a rainbow will streak across the sky, reminding us of God's promise."

Wentworth scowled, and she laughed, the sound rippling through him, creating the warmest feeling he'd ever had on the inside. He came up on his elbows. "It is much more…romantic than that."

"So, tell me," she said, a lovely smile playing about her mouth.

"Sir Isaac Newton studied the *phenomenon of colors. He was the first to understand that the beautiful array of colors we see is not from a* mixture of light and darkness as proposed by Aristotle, but that sunlight contained all colors which could be separated by prisms. Whenever white light is refracted with a prism, we see colors. The sun actually creates rainbows when sunlight passes through raindrops. The raindrops act like tiny prisms. They bend the different colors in white light, so the light spreads out into a band of colors that are reflected back to us as a rainbow."

Her smile widened. "Ah, so now you have explained how Our Lord did it, but I told you the why. Is it not beautiful?"

Wentworth stared, then he smiled. "You are beautiful. I am going to kiss you…"

Her eyes widened, and she lifted slightly off the earth to glance around. "I do not think it would go over well, should another of your staff see you kissing your valet!"

He shifted, leaning over her, his body blotting the low sun from her face.

"I dreamed of kissing you," he murmured, "and I woke with the taste of you still on my mouth. How is that possible?"

She cleared her throat, her blush getting brighter. "Is that not a common occurrence?"

"Not for me," he immediately replied. "And I've kissed other ladies before."

They stared at each other, and he removed the hat from her face, and was tempted to remove the wig.

"What is that look on your face," she said softly, her eyes searching his expression. "I've never seen you appear so intense, and I've seen you walk into a door before because you were so engrossed with reading."

"Saw that, did you?"

She touched the corner of his mouth with a gloved finger. "I did."

"I am a gentleman," he began.

"I know."

"I've never seduced an innocent before."

The corner of her eyes crinkled with her smile. "Is that what you're about? Seduction?"

"Well, I am thinking of kissing you until we are both senseless."

"I sense an objection."

"A gentleman does not take advantage of a young lady unless he knows he will marry her," he said gruffly. "How can I kiss you…do all the things I hunger to do without making you my wife? I would be a right rogue."

She slipped her hands around his neck, and he braced himself on his elbows. And they just stared at each other. In her eyes, he spied something tender and wicked.

"That means I am a rogue as well because I want you to kiss me more than anything else."

"Juliana—" he began warningly.

"And I do not want you to marry me when you are done." This, she said with amusement dancing in her lovely lavender eyes. "Marriage is not a part of my plan, and it is silly for you to have it in your thoughts."

"That sounds as if you are granting me the liberty to act a rogue, Miss Pryce."

"And if I am?" she asked teasingly.

"Then you had best be prepared to deal with the corollary effects."

"A few kisses are hardly something to worry over."

Her words were bold, but her eyes bright with curiosity and longing. A mischievous anticipation shivered through his heart and trailed down to his cock. He tugged the gloves from his hands, now braced above her, desperate to feel the softness of her skin beneath his fingertips. "Silly, Miss Pryce...a few kisses? Rogues and scoundrels do not stop at kisses, only the most stalwart of gentlemen do."

Juliana caught her breath at his implication, a flush warming her cheeks. "How shocking, even with that knowledge, I want your kisses."

Wentworth took her mouth with his, pressing in for a very thorough and naughty kiss. She moaned, the sound so achy and bloody sweet. His heart started to pound, and he reverently cupped her jaw, sliding his thumb to the fluttering pulse at her throat. And he took her mouth in a wet, carnal claiming, sliding his tongue along her bottom lip, and when she parted her mouth, his tongue ravished her.

Wentworth had never felt such raw need from a kiss. Something roared inside of him, urging him to wrench her trousers down, right here in the open, lick along her wet slit and then take her with long, deep strokes.

His cock throbbed, and with a harsh groan, he released her mouth, kissing down to her arched neck. The kiss he pressed into the hollow of her throat was violent with restrained hunger. He reached between them, tugging her shirt from her trousers. Soon the skin of her belly was bare to his touch.

Her breath caught in her throat as his hand stroked over the lowest part of her abdomen. His hand ran lightly up and down her quivery soft stomach, his touch lingering and provocative. Wentworth went even lower, slipping his fingers below the waistband of her trousers. They both faltered into stillness, the provocative intimacy of the moment creating a subtle tension in their bodies.

His fingers grazed her mons, the soft hair curling there. A tiny whimper slipped from Juliana, and she grasped his shoulders.

"Remove your gloves, I want your bare hands on me."

She complied and tossed them onto the grass. When she touched him next, it was to cup his cheeks. How delicate her fingers felt…how soft! With a groan, he lowered his head and kissed her. This time slowly, savoring each sigh and breathy moan she made against his lips.

Desire knifed through him, sharp and insistent. Her hips lifted in entreaty, but he did not move the fingers lightly rested on her mons. If he dared move them, slipped them lower and found her wet…

His cock jerked, and he pulled his mouth from hers, also removing his hand from her body and tugging her shirt down. Her lips were red, and it would be evident to anyone with eyes that they had been thoroughly kissed.

He touched his thumb to her damp, swollen lips. If she was a debutante, and they had been caught alone together like this on his grass, he would be honor-bound to marry her. Yet Juliana didn't want marriage. He understood that. It simply wasn't a part of her plan, and the feelings burgeoning between them were too new, too unfamiliar for it to interfere with the long-held dreams she had of her future.

Hell, he shouldn't even be thinking of her and marriage in the same breath. Yet Wentworth knew that he liked her a lot. And he had five more weeks with her under his roof. It would be impossible to resist kissing her *and* doing more. Yet it felt damn wrong to ask her to be his mistress.

But what about a friend…and a lover?

He rolled off her, lying flat on his back again, wondering if the distinction between a lover and a mistress would make him less of a scoundrel. On the one hand, he helped her maintained her ruse because he wanted her safe and her charade was harmless. If she were to remove her disguise, word of a young marriageable lady under his roof would travel swiftly around the parish and might even reach London. Those damn busybodies and their gossiping mouths.

"I can feel you thinking," she murmured.

"I am wondering at the smartness of you acting as my valet for several more weeks. Perhaps I was too hasty with the suggestion."

"Are you thinking of the scandal should I be discovered?"

Before he could reply, she asked another question, this

time with a quaver in her tone. "Do you wish me to leave, my lord?"

"No. The very opposite. I greatly like your company."

He felt her pleasure as if she had touched him.

He placed his hands behind his head. "The chances of your stepfather finding you here are very slim. Even if you were to stay as Miss Juliana Pryce, a guest in my home."

"Do you really think he might hear of it should I remain as a guest?"

"People gossip. But I did a quick analysis of the people we know, grouped them, and created an intersection. The probability of him uncovering that you are under my roof if you remain as yourself is about five percent."

"And what would I do if he discovered me?"

"Nothing. You are a guest in my home. He cannot just take you. I would not allow it."

"I would never want to endanger you!" she gasped.

"I am an earl of the realm, I rank above your stepfather, so it is no danger. But if he acts the boor, I will challenge the man to a duel. I am an expert fencer and a crack shot. If he refuses, I'll probably plant him a facer for frightening you with his kidnapping and chasing after you. But he'll understand that you are protected."

"You are entirely serious," she said.

"Of course."

"You would fight a duel…punch my stepfather if he dared to come for me here?"

Wentworth once again shifted his head on the grass and their gazes collided. "Of course. I am a good fighter. Not many in society know that I've fought in the fighting pits."

A garbled sound of shock emitted from her, and he scowled.

"You've fought in a fighting pit...in the barbaric manner of bare-knuckle boxing?"

"Yes."

"Good heavens!" she said in admiring tones. "You *are* a man of many talents."

He nodded smugly, pleased with her admiration. "That I am. And I even won a purse of five thousand pounds some weeks ago."

She smiled, but it slowly dimmed. "I am that poor of a valet?"

He leaned in, his lips almost touching hers. "Only a saint could resist taking you to his bed."

Juliana's breath hitched audibly. She met his eyes, and she swallowed. "And you are not a saint."

Her words were barely audible.

"I am no saint, but a man who is *very* attracted to an exceptionally pretty lady."

You were warned, seemed to float silently from his thoughts to hers. But instead of blushing and looking away as he'd anticipated, she smiled, reached over, and laced their hands together.

❦

IT HOVERED on Juliana's tongue to tell Wentworth that she wanted more than kisses with him, but once again, that odd shyness assailed her, and she silently sighed. *I do not want you to stop at kisses.* The caress against her bare stomach just now had aroused her senses to startling heights. How she had ached, and even now her skin felt sensitized, her breasts heavy, her face flushed.

"I prefer to remain as your valet," Juliana said. "If I were to appear as Miss Pryce, your mother and aunt would expect me to be a paragon of ladylike behavior. As Julian, I am free to come and go without scrutiny."

"Very well, we shall not speak of it again then. But know I'll not allow your stepfather or anyone to take you before your five and twentieth birthday."

The feelings swirling inside her chest were sweet and fierce and hungry. Juliana hoped they would never leave, but was also perplexed on what to do with them. How she wished he had not rolled off her. His large presence had been comforting, even as it had roused her senses.

I am so wanton, she thought with a measure of amusement.

"I suspect you want the freedom to move about freely."

"Yes."

"Though we are in the country, it is best to always walk with protection. If you mean to traverse the woods, take one of the dogs with you or even a pistol."

"I will," she said, then offered, knowing he must have wondered where she had gone for so long. "I visited Billy today."

"The boy who'd been hunting on my lands?"

"Yes."

Wentworth frowned thoughtfully. "You went to check up on him?"

"Yes. I…I just wanted to see if he got the job with your game master and if Billy's family was doing well."

"I see. And is he well?"

"He's not gone to the game master as yet. He was worried about his clothes. They were very rag tagged. And his shoes had holes in them. His mother works as a washerwoman in the parish, and they can barely afford to clothe themselves for the winter. He knows he has to present as respectable to work under the gamekeeper at the Earl of Rawlings's estate."

"I will pay them a visit," he said gruffly. "And take him directly to Mr. Colby."

Her stepfather would have been affronted at the very idea. Yet Wentworth did not hesitate to offer to pay this family a visit. "They are not your tenants," she said softly, "They rent a very run-down cottage from Squire Harris. He does not maintain their abode because they are behind on rent. I suppose it is a kindness he allowed them to stay for the last few months, but I suspect he might fancy the lady's eldest daughter. She is fourteen and a beauty."

Quickly she relayed to Wentworth, her impression of the girl. Juliana had spent some time talking to her while they walked in the woods. She had been incredibly careful not to appear a suitor and listened to the girl's dream to be a seamstress. However, to procure the money to start that journey seemed impossible, unless she relied on the squire who had slyly offered to assist the young girl's endeavors.

"Bloody hell," Wentworth growled. "The man is known for his profligacy about town. How did you help?"

She dug her fingers into the grass. "Why did you think I helped?"

He chuffed. "I might have only known you for a week, but you are a lady of thoughtful manners and kindness."

Juliana grinned. "I had to sell a necklace of mine to

make some purchases for my ruse. I had some money left over. I…I gave Billy's mother a hundred pounds in banknotes."

Julian's throat ached when she recalled the lady's shock and the tears. "Her dignity was upset, so she tried to refuse it, but Billy took it for her."

"Smart lad."

"They are a family of six. That money will keep them well fed for several months, buy them suitable clothes and new boots for the winter. And also bring them current on their rent, and perhaps even pay for another year. It really astonishes me the disparity of wealth between the upper and lower society. Did you know that as your valet, my wage is thirty pounds per year? That one-hundred-pounds is roughly three years' salary for me. And I am a top paid servant in your household."

"I will inform my land steward in the morning to increase all my servant's wages appropriately, and I will give each a considerable bonus this year."

Juliana laughed, delighted with him. "I even thought of a business that might help young girls like Laura. Perhaps a charity of sorts that will fund their apprenticeship for at least three years. Each person would receive the funds to pay for independent lodgings, food, and the work tools they might need for the duration needed to learn their skills. Or perhaps a school of sort…that teaches these skills to these young ladies, and provide lodgings, food, and even a stipend."

"A worthy endeavor," he murmured, a smile touching his mouth. "Many will try to fraudulently take the money and run. It would need to be administered and would cost as much in administration."

"Have I mentioned that my inheritance from my father is an obscene amount."

"I imagined you to be like most England heiress with fifty thousand pounds or more."

"A mere pittance," she drawled. "But that would be a worthy business investment were I to remain in England."

He stiffened, and something undefinable flashed in his eyes. "You have thought of staying?"

The air around them felt altered, and her heart clamored. "I...I've not given it any thoughts really; it was a slip of the tongue. I...I would not need to be present for such a business to start."

He looked away, shuttering away the intensity. Was it that he wanted her to stay in England? That couldn't be it; he'd just made her acquaintance. Juliana did not understand the sudden pounding ache that went through her heart. "Wentworth—"

"I will be going to London soon. You are to remain here at Norbrook Park."

An odd sensation dropped low in her belly. "You are leaving?"

"Only for a few days."

"And I am to remain here...without you?"

"That is what I said."

"But a valet always travels with his master. Will it not be odd?"

"You staying here also lessens the potential conflict of encountering your stepfather and risking recognition. I do not believe there is another lady in all of England with your eyes. Or a lad for that matter."

Juliana had nothing to say to that, but she felt like hugging him to her and then kissing him. Even her brother called her eyes strange, other people said odd, but Wentworth said beautiful and unique. "Why are you going?"

A singularly bold question when she had no claim on his time or pursuits. An awful thought occurred to her. "Is it to your mistress?"

The eyes that looked at her gleamed with an emotion she could not decipher. "So, you think I have the makings of a rogue, to be wanting you desperately in my bed, but go to London to tup another woman?"

Juliana blushed and sat up on the grass. "I do not know why I said that." *Wanting you desperately in my bed.*

He snorted, but it was more a sound of amusement. "I am going to buy a dress, dancing shoes, and a mask for a certain lady to attend a ball to be held here at Norbrook Park in a couple weeks."

Me. She couldn't help the smile that bloomed on her lips. "Why a masked ball?"

"Once you leave Norbrook Park, it is unlikely we will see each other again."

Her heart gave a frightful squeeze. Unexpectedly, the very idea felt unbearable. "You could visit me in New York," she said with a soft smile.

"Hmm, and I am certain you will revisit England. But when will these magical visits happen? A few years from now?"

She pulled a few pieces of grass and tossed them toward the lake.

"At the ball, I want to see you in a pretty dress, dancing slippers, and with flowers in your hair. I want to hold you in my arms and dance with you for the entire night, for I might never get the chance again."

And I want that too.

"I'll brush up on my dancing then, I've not had much practice." Looking out toward the lake, she said, "I would entrust to you a letter for my mother. She is in Bath at Camden Place and entirely unaware of what my stepfather has done. I do not want to alarm her if she does not know, but I must send her a letter to let her know I am staying with a few friends. I'll be suitably vague about my whereabouts, but she will know that I am well."

"I will arrange it for you."

"Thank you, Wentworth."

He fisted the back of her jacket and tugged her down, so she fell atop him.

"Tonight, I'm going to serve you."

"With kisses?" she murmured, brushing her mouth against his.

"I am going to give you a bath in my chamber…and then towel you off."

She froze at the provocative image that blasted in her mind. "You'll do no such thing," Juliana gasped.

He arched a brow. "So, you've taken a bath since you've been here? I do not think so. You've only been using a washbasin with tepid water. Anything more would risk the other staff discovering you. Imagine it," the devil tempted. "That large copper tub, filled with hot water, a rose-scented soap, and you soak as long as you wish. I'll even help you wash your hair."

She moaned, and he closed his eyes, a shudder going through his body.

"Make that sound again."

Juliana blinked, uncertain how to reproduce the sound; it had been natural and simply slipped out. Wanting to please him, she tried. It sounded like a dying frog.

He grinned, then laughed. The sound of his laughter was rich and husky. She liked it. "You—"

"My lord!" a high pitch voice squeaked in abject shock.

They froze, and Juliana barely shifted her head to see a small lad of about ten years, just staring at them, his eyes wide in his face.

"What are you doing here, boy?"

"I…I…mi…I…" The boy grunted, clearly flustered and frustrated with getting his words out. "Swim!" he finally said, still staring at the sight of a supposed gentleman atop his master.

"What is your name?"

"Tommy, milord!"

"And where do you work?"

"In…in the stables with me pa," he said proudly.

She could feel Wentworth thinking.

"I forbid you from telling anyone what you've seen today."

"Yes, milord!"

"Good, now run along."

The boy disappeared, and Juliana blew out a sharp breath. Before she could speak, a voice said,

"Milord?"

"Bloody hell," Wentworth said, "I thought you left, Tommy."

"Yes, milord, but me came back. What ye mean by forbid?"

"I am your master, and you are not to tell anyone you saw me with my valet lying atop me."

There was a thoughtful silence, and she looked up to see the boy staring at her.

"I didn't know he was yer valet, milord. I thought it was a girl dressed as a lad. Shan't tell a soul, milord!"

Wentworth reached into his pocket, withdrew a coin, and flicked it at the boy. His eyes went wide at the sum, and a toothy grin spread across his face before he took off.

It was to her credit that she kept a straight face until the lad disappeared. Juliana dissolved into laughter.

"I am uncertain what there's to laugh about," Wentworth grumbled.

Despite his disgruntlement, laughter lurked in his tone.

"You should have seen the look on your face. Do you think young Tommy will gossip with the other servants?"

"He's young, and he bloody well thought you a girl until I put other ideas in his head. How was I fooled, and the lad knew it with one look? No doubt it was your lush derriere that did the trick."

"My derriere?" she asked archly.

"Hmm, it was this sweetly rounded mouthwatering backside of yours which first roused me...in every way."

Juliana chuckled even harder. Wentworth spun with her, bracing his weight above her.

In his eyes, she spied something tender.

"Your laughter sounds like a goose."

How did he manage to infuse such beguiling warmth into his voice? It took her a moment, but she gasped. "I do not!"

He grinned, leaned down, and kissed her. With a sweet sigh of contentment, she wrapped her hands around his neck and returned his kiss, wishing for the first time she could stay in England.

CHAPTER 11

Four days later, Juliana slipped inside the earl's room. Since learning of her identity, he hardly required her to assist him, and Wentworth appeared just as well-groomed as he had been before. She still dealt with pressing his clothes and polishing his shoes, but that did not fill her days. Each evening she stood behind him at the dining table and observed him as he laughed and chatted with his family. His mother had a quick wit, and Juliana found her delightful. His Aunt Millicent seemed a bit sterner, yet she glowed with good-natured warmth and indulged her twin daughters to a degree Juliana considered excessive. They discussed everything, their neighbors and the latest gossip, politics, news from abroad, next year's season, and eligible ladies they suggested for Wentworth as prospective brides.

Hearing his mother stating how happy she was that her son was finally bride hunting created a stabbing pain in Juliana's heart. The reaction was ludicrous and out of bounds for what was acceptable for their relationship. But that was it, wasn't it? She didn't understand the bounds of their odd friendship that simmered with such wanting.

We do not have a relationship. We have…nothing…everything, laughter, and such ease of comfort in each other's presence.

Each night she would enter his bedroom after dinner to help him remove his boots and jacket, despite knowing he did not require her help. Each night she knew the bathtub waited for her. Still, she ignored it, knowing he watched her with tender amusement and something else, something unknown gleaming in the depth of his gaze. That something else always had an answering surge going through her body. Still, she could not identify what his eyes spoke of and what part of her responded?

Was it just desire? Or something deeper?

After removing his boots and jacket, they would lie entangled by the fire, her head on his chest, her arm hugging him, and her leg touching or thrown across his. If she had been curious about anything they gossiped about, she would ask him, he would explain it to her, and she would laugh and bask in the contentment of the moment.

There had been another night when they had played chess.

Then last night, she had reposed with her head in his lap while he read Sir Isaac Newton's Law on Motions aloud to her. How delighted he had been whenever she understood a section. How eagerly and with such remarkable insight he'd clarified whatever she had not understood.

It was not long since she'd first hidden at Norbrook Park, and Juliana couldn't understand it, but in Wentworth, it felt like she had found something rare and so very precious. Now she stood in the center of Wentworth's room, a slight trembling within her body. She was uncertain whether it was from nerves or anticipation. Her reckless heart declared it was with excitement.

Let me serve you.

As if she would allow him in the room when she took that bath. A silent affirmation Juliana repeated each night. Except tonight, she turned toward the bath chamber and stared, her heart pounding. The room was barely lit by a roaring fire, and a few candle tapers set around it. There was a pleasant scent redolent in the air, and she followed it to the luxurious bath chamber. The large copper tub was filled with steaming water, with rose petals floating on the surface.

On the peg near the entrance hung a bathrobe. The material was an icy blue, and so sheer Julianna flushed. Did he hope she would wear it? Towels had been placed on a wash stool with a bar of soap. Picking it up, she inhaled, breathing in the scent of perfumed roses. The door behind her opened, and her heart jumped a beat. Juliana sensed the earl entering the bath chamber with a thrill of expectancy. There was that strange flutter low in her belly and she felt elated.

"Your bath awaits you, my lady," he murmured, husky mischief lifting his tone.

She couldn't say what madness seized her, but she reached up and removed the wig and dropped it to the floor. "And you'll help me wash my hair?" she murmured softly.

The earl's response was a sharp intake of breath. And she knew then he had intended to play the gentleman, not the rogue. He had not anticipated her answer, even though he had teasingly prepared the tub nightly. So many warm feelings crashed against her senses. Juliana removed her neck cloth, jacket, and undershirt. Next, she drew off her boots, trousers, and stockings, until she stood only in her drawers and the bindings around her breasts.

"I'll turn away," he said hoarsely.

He sounded like a man dying of thirst. No man had ever desired her so blatantly. Juliana had always believed her lack of voluptuous curves would not tempt any man. The most particular compliment she'd ever received was that she had a lovely smile. Most comments she received were about the unusual color of her lavender-blue eyes, criticisms of her skin's olive blush from her love of spending time outdoors, and snide remarks on the darkness of her hair.

But Wentworth made her feel utterly beautiful. She felt a sharp pinch in her chest. "I remember someone saying I had the sweetest backside he'd ever seen…you would turn away and miss seeing it unclothed?"

"No," he groaned, with noticeable relief.

And with trembling fingers, and thousands of birds fluttering in her stomach, she undid the bindings, then untied the tapes of her drawers.

"*Bloody hell*," he spat, almost reverently.

Then there was nothing more said, just a breathless, aching silence. The quiet almost made her squirm. She could feel his desire urging her to turn around, but he did not voice his hopes. She wasn't ready to turn around yet. Lifting her hand to her hair, she removed the pins, letting them clatter to the floor. Her wavy tresses tumbled to her shoulders and down to her breasts. Juliana walked forward and stepped into the tub, a sigh of delight slipping from her.

How had she gone without a bath for so long?

She lowered herself into the large tub, giggling to see that it swallowed her petite frame. The water came up to her chin, and the heat of it enveloped her body. Holding her breath, she slid lower, covering her head for several seconds. Juliana resurfaced with a sigh of bliss.

"Are you still going to help me wash my hair?" Juliana asked, reaching for the rose-scented soap and rubbing it along her throat and over her arms.

The rustle of sounds implied the earl was undressing, and her heart raced at such speed she felt faint. The temptation to turn around and watch him beat at her senses, but she held fast, soaping her body thoroughly, even slipping her hand beneath the water to her womanly center.

A hiss echoed in the bath chamber.

Wentworth hadn't been preoccupied with removing his clothes; he still observed her. Heat swept along Juliana's body, and she tried to move efficiently.

"Do it slower," he said gruffly.

In the silence that followed his words, they were both very still.

"You cannot see," she finally pointed out, aware of her entire body burning red.

"I can see the motion of your shoulders…and my imagination is healthy and very much active. I want it slower."

Juliana licked her lips that had gone dry, reaching for

the soft washcloth on the small table. She lathered it, leaned back her head, and coasted the washcloth from her throat down to the space between her breasts, over her trembling belly, and to her aching sex. There she slowly and carefully parted her sex, rubbing the cloth over her folds in a way she had never done before.

At his lack of response, she peeked around, and amusement wafted through her. The earl stood with his head tipped to the ceiling, a palm pressed against his forehead, his expression a tight grimace of arousal. He dropped his hand and looked at her. Wentworth stood with bare feet, only in his trousers, his naked chest on delightful display. Juliana allowed herself to make a leisured perusal of his charms. Her eyes wandered over the sculptured perfection of his body, emotions flittered through his eyes, reflected in the glass of his spectacles. She saw desire, hunger, admiration, and awe all fettered by a determined will. A will that was failing to suppress his very obvious arousal. When her eyes returned to his glasses, his lips twitched.

"The better to see you with, my dear," he drawled with a sensual smile that was *felt* inside her belly and even lower.

Juliana stared at him as if seeing him for the first time. There was nothing soft on him, anywhere. "I am ready to wash my hair," she murmured.

He padded over, took up the rose-scented soap, and kneeled behind her. Much in the manner she had done when she'd washed his shoulders. Wentworth took the washcloth, and it was Juliana's turn to grip the edges of the bathtub as he swiped it gently across her back, shoulders, and around to her belly.

What was this hot, aching sensation throbbing at the very core of her body?

Swapping the perfumed soap for a plain bar, he lathered her hair. He worked his fingers into it, massaging her scalp, unaware of the breathless anticipation building in the air. He did it even better than the lady's maid she often shared with her mother. A few minutes later, her hair was cleansed, and while she stood, he poured warm water over her head and down her body. She felt his presence withdrew, and Juliana turned to see him standing near the entrance to the bath chamber, his back to her.

He fascinated her. Wentworth did not overpower or hammer at her resistance. That would have probably sent her running despite the longing crawling through her body. In all her four and twenty years, she had never felt like *this*, and Julianna suspected it might never happen again. Such likings must be a rarity, and she had been lucky enough to find it in the most unlikely place.

No, her earl did not overwhelm her senses; his sensual threat was subtle, the lure to sweet recklessness insidious. He was scandalously in her presence while she bathed, yet he did not look at her body unless invited. When she rose from the bath, he looked away, giving her time to towel dry.

A gentleman *and* a rogue. Juliana smiled, wanting him even more. She hadn't known she was capable of such dangerous self-indulgence. After patting dry her body, and most of the wetness from her hair, she slipped on the silken night robe. It clung to the moist places on her body and whispered around her feet in shimmering waves. Her hair tumbled to her shoulders in a mass of damp curls, which dripped the occasional droplet onto the night-wrap.

He walked ahead of her, and she followed him.

"Sleep in here with me tonight."

Juliana swallowed tightly. "I…am here being so very liberal, Wentworth, but I am not ready to…to…," she whispered, blushing.

"I know you are not ready for me to take you."

Her heart beat violently. *How did he know?*

"Come here."

She sauntered over to where he stood by the fire.

He lifted her chin with a finger. "It was an invitation; one you can reject."

"I know," she whispered. This man would never force her to do anything she did not want.

"I am leaving for London tomorrow…and tonight, I…" He lifted a shoulder. "I simply wanted you near. I will rest my head on the chaise."

"That bed can sleep five people comfortably."

He stilled. "You'll stay."

"Yes. It's been days since you last kissed me."

Anticipation leaped in his eyes. "Only kisses tonight… but let me tell you, these kisses will be shockingly scandalous. But if you do not want them, there is no problem."

"I want them," she gasped, knowing she was walking a dangerous edge.

"Lie down on the bed. I want to look at you. Do not take off the peignoir…but allow it to part, so I might see the shadows of your breasts…the hollow of your belly and that dark thatch of hair shielding the place I desperately want to taste."

She expelled a breath. "With your mouth?"

The image of the earl kissing her between her thighs was shocking *and* terribly arousing. And not what he meant, surely.

"Yes. With my mouth…and tongue."

All she heard was the sudden roar of blood in her veins. Juliana walked away and sat on the bed with a plop, very inelegant, but it was as if the power of his words felled her.

I want that.

A pool of heat settled low in her belly. Tugging the slim tie at the front of the robe…or peignoir as he called it, she allowed it to part slightly so he could peek at her naked body. She blushed when his gaze settled on the hint of her breasts revealed. Her almost non-existent breasts.

Yet his gaze, intense and heavy-lidded, revealed an expression of utmost satisfaction. He visibly shuddered, and the bulge at the front of his trousers became considerably larger. It swept through her then, feminine power, a sense of awe that he should react to her in such a way. As if he too was helpless under the sweeping desire pervading through her body. Juliana leaned back, her elbows dropping to the mattress, and slinked her body up to the center of the bed.

A purr of hungry approval slipped from him, and he padded over to her. She was so very wicked tempting him to ravish her, yet Juliana never felt safer.

He knew she was not ready to take that final leap and make love with him. Each time she thought about it, she got flustered. However, Wentworth allowed her to be wanton…free…teasing…and he remained a gentleman. The trust that she felt for him felt like an invisible tether, drawing them closer together.

"Give me one of your feet."

That she did not expect, but she lifted a foot in the air and rested it against his chest. The silk of her nightgown fell toward her thighs, but his gaze did not leave the arch of her feet.

"What delicate ankles you have."

He lifted her foot higher, and to her shock, he kissed right above her ankle. The heat of his mouth against her flesh was unexpected but very nice. More than nice. More kisses to her calf, up to the side of her knees. As he revealed a piece of her body by peeling away the silk gown, he would kiss a spot. Soon he tugged her to sit up in the bed, pushing the robe from her shoulders.

Wentworth gathered her hair to one side so he could press a kiss to her nape. He kissed her cheek, her lips, her chin: delicate licks and small nips. Wentworth kissed the hollow of her throat and teased his teeth over her fluttering pulse. Then he went to her shoulders, he kissed her inner elbows, and then he was at her breasts.

There he worshipped with his tongue and teeth until she was a writhing mess. The nipple he had between his teeth ached, but it was such a pleasurable one. She cried out weakly when he sucked one of her nipples deep into his mouth. The pull felt right at that place between her thighs, which seemed like it had a heartbeat of its own. She throbbed. She was wet. So incredibly wet, and he hadn't touched her there with his fingers or even his promised mouth.

He went down, and he kissed her navel. Restless with hunger, she shimmered down, not willing to just be a receiver of the tormenting pleasure but a participant. Juliana touched his face with her fingertips. Traced his mouth with trembling fingers. Kissed his throat as he'd done hers, licking over his pulse, lingering there until she felt his heartbeat inside her. Then she gently bit.

His body jolted, and he gripped her hips almost painfully. She kissed his shoulders. Wentworth hadn't stopped touching her, and he traced the bridge of her nose with his fingertip, his touch light and sensual down to the hollow of her cheek, and the shape of her bottom lip. Juliana reacted with carnal instincts and a pure craving to weaken him with kisses as he devastated her.

She kissed the pad of his finger, then sucked it into her mouth.

Wentworth groaned, ripped the rest of the sheer nightgown from her body, and pressed her down into the soft bed on her stomach. Teeth sank into her buttocks. She arched, a wail slipping from her at the sensation. He kissed down to the shadows of her thighs, and her entire body trembled.

He crawled over her, the power of his body covering her like a warm sensual blanket. That hard place between his thighs rested against her derriere. Juliana was dazedly aware that sweat slicked her skin, though he still retained his trousers. The feel of the material against her skin was at once arousing and provoking.

"Wentworth," she gasped when he pushed a hand

underneath her hips and arched her buttocks up. Then she felt the imprint of his arousal like a searing brand.

His lips were close to her ear. "Juliana." Then a kiss to her nape, and a soft bite into her shoulder blade.

His breathing, too, was shallow and irregular.

She turned her face, sliding her cheek against smooth sheets. The position he had her in felt evocative and almost intimidating. He shifted her slightly so he could reach her mouth. His kiss was a slow, intimate knowing of her mouth, and she sobbed her relief to be tasting him. He tasted sweet of wine and berries and of the man himself. She sucked on his tongue, bit into his bottom lips, nipped at his chin, and when he laughed, the sound was rough and sensual.

Juliana never imagined desire could be this desperate and hungry.

The knowledge sank into her bones then. She was petrified that if she gifted him her body, the feelings swelling inside her now would worsen, and she would betray all the dreams and plans she'd made with her brother for this passion.

How silly could she be? A sob hitched in her throat. The fire ignited deeper in her belly. Her skin was sensitized, and everywhere ached. Wentworth turned her over gently and went upon his knees, peering down at her.

"Let me see your quim."

Her legs scandalously fell open to his heated gaze until her sex was lushly on display.

"What a pretty quim you have," he said softly, reaching out as if he would touch her there.

At the last minute, he stopped, and an ache of need pierced low in her belly.

"No touching," he reminded, "and I am a gentleman of my word."

"You promised me your mouth…*there*."

He dropped to his knees off the bed and stuffed two pillows below her hips. Juliana almost laughed, unable to imagine what it would be like to stare at him in the morning. After every salacious act they were doing now.

Wanton debauchery…and I am such a happy participant!

She stilled when his breath wafted against the heated folds of her sex. Juliana thought he would have tortured her with more teasing licks before kissing her there, but she was wrong, and she gripped the sheets as he went right for her throbbing center.

Her heart beat so loudly in her ears as she waited for what must be the wickedest act between a man and his lady. All of Juliana's awareness narrowed on the delicate, excruciatingly light stroke of his tongue over her aching sex. That was just a teasing foray, for with a groan, he licked her with decadent greed.

Juliana scream under the hot lash of his tongue, fisting the sheets as pleasure burned her alive. It rushed through her like a tempest, and she burst apart with bliss as her body peaked.

"Again," he said, flicking that sensitive bundle of nerves.

"I do not think I can…. Argh!" her wail was one of agonized bliss as he sucked her nub of pleasure in his mouth with strong pulls. She came up on the bed, arching on her elbows, her head thrown back as her thighs started to shake.

Juliana felt hot, and weak, and almost scared at the pulsating sensation where his mouth pleasured. Again, she splintered apart. And again, and again, until she collapsed weakly onto the bed.

He disappeared for a few minutes, then returned with the washcloth and cleaned between her legs. Juliana blushed, but she hadn't the energy to protest. He lay beside her, and she curled into his side, noting how raggedly he still breathed and the tension in his frame.

She'd seen so little of his body. She wanted to touch him, study him, pleasure him as he had pleased her. He was so unselfish, taking her to heights of bliss several times but denying himself any release. She would have admired his control if not for the pained expression of unfulfilled passion.

"You will be unable to sleep," she murmured.

"That is a very distinct possibility."

"Let me pleasure you."

His low chuckle felt strained. "Get dressed and meet me outside in a few minutes."

Pressing a kiss to her forehead, he pushed from the bed and started to dress. It took Juliana a few minutes before she could move her well-satiated body. After quickly dressing and meeting Wentworth in the hallway, they stood on a bluff on his estate several minutes later. There lay a large blanket on the grass, and a telescope was set upon its tripod and a table. She wondered what the footmen who set it up had thought.

"When did you do this?"

He smiled. "I confess I ordered this set up earlier before I knew the delights that awaited me in my chamber."

She laughed, annoyed she once again flushed.

"I thought we could stargaze and drink together." He lifted his chin toward the decanter on the blanket.

"No wine glasses?" she said, arching a brow at the decanter he was lying beside.

"We are living on the edge of reason tonight."

"How dangerous, to drink directly from the flask." She reached out, indicating toward the bottle. This would be the first time she had ever drunk directly from a flask. How scandalous.

He laughed and tugged her down beside him, fitting her perfectly into his side. The feeling of his arms around her was a revelation. *I belong in your arms.*

"Juliana?"

"Yes?"

She waited for him to explain how he planned to show her the wonders of the night sky.

"I am falling in love with you."

Fright gripped her heart only to be chased away by a fierce rush of joy. "Wentworth—"

"I only wanted you to know," he said softly, his eyes caressing over her face with quiet intensity. "You matter to me...greatly."

"I...you…" She looked away into the sky. She snatched the decanter and took her first swig in what felt like the most inelegant fashion.

"What?" he asked with some amusement.

She lowered her head to gaze at him searchingly. "I

was just thinking you…you are the gentleman I hadn't known I was searching for."

"So, you'll marry me then?"

She dropped the decanter of wine, and he snatched it out of the air with his quick reflexes.

A breathtaking smile tugged at the corners of his lips. "Should I ask?"

Juliana stared at him in astonishment. "I cannot see an earl as important as yourself, leaving England to live in New York."

He looked away, down the rolling valley for a long time.

"Do you not enjoy living in England?"

She searched for the right words. "We moved here two years after my father died. That was four years ago. Mama could not stay in New York, where every memory of papa made her inconsolable. She was originally from Wiltshire, you know. Papa visited England after the Napoleonic wars to seek new business ventures. He said the first time he saw mama; she was in a meadow picking flowers. She looked up, smiling, and he fell in love with her." Juliana laughed, recalling fondly the whimsical nature of her father. The very one her mother had sworn her daughter also possessed. "She returned home, a wealthy businessman's widow, and caught the eye of Viscount Bramley."

She reached for the decanter and took another sip directly from the flask.

"And they married."

"Yes. Mama fell in love again, and I daresay the Viscount was also a man enamored of her, even if he is a cretin for wanting my inheritance. I was only meant to stay in England for a year, then it turned into another, and then another. I have not been home in four years."

"I can hear the longing in your voice," he said softly. "Is New York beautiful then?"

"Yes, and also different from the bustle of London but very much similar. I think you would enjoy it there."

They sat there on the grass, staring into the night sky for long silent moments.

"Tomorrow, I leave for Town. I believe I shall miss you, Miss Pryce."

She smiled. "I know for a certainty that I will miss you, Wentworth."

He turned, shifted over to her, and went up on his elbow. Wentworth lowered his head and pressed his mouth to hers in a tender, devastating kiss that reached inside her and tore at her heart.

I am falling in love with you, too, she offered silently, sweetly returning his kiss with all the emotions brewing in her heart.

Oh, what am I to do?

CHAPTER 12

"I've never known you to appear this contemplative when your nose wasn't in a book," Michael, Viscount Worsley murmured. "You, my friend, have been rather inattentive about the large sum of money you are about to lose."

Wentworth sighed, lowering his cards to the tabletop.

"And that sound could have only been inspired by a woman, do tell," his friend said, his voice a rich purr. "I've never seen you so distracted at the club before, you normally come to win and bleed me dry."

Wentworth chuckled, leaning back in his chair, and tossed back his brandy. His friend owned a gambling hell called The Club. It was more than just operating this den of iniquity which had given him the moniker Viscount Wicked. It was his manner with the ladies who continually offered themselves up for his ravishment. Their friendship was unorthodox because they were truly so different, 'the saintly scholar' and the 'viscount wicked' as their other friends liked to mockingly call them.

"Is it truly a woman has you so out of sorts?" the viscount demanded. "I would have lost the wager if I'd said that no lady could ever control all of your interest."

Wentworth refilled his glass and took another careful sip. "I am thinking about my valet. I have been in town for three days and I am bloody haunted. I can barely sleep, nor can I erase the taste…" With a groan he tipped back his head to stare in the ceiling. "Michael, I fear I am going mad from want."

Worsley paused in lighting his cheroot, carefully containing his expression. His silver eyes however danced with deviltry. "I never knew you leaned toward—"

"Good God, man, my valet is a woman in disguise."

"How…fascinating." He pulled on his cheroot. "Any lady I know?"

"As if I would reveal her identity."

His friend grinned. "Such opportunities you have for debauchery, my friend. A lady in your private quarters. Tell me all the details."

"There is nothing to tell, I've been a damned gentleman." Except…bloody hell, except for the night before he'd left. The taste of her, the feel of her under his hand, that lush derriere in his hand and rubbing against his cock. How had he resisted? Her smile when they star gazed. That tenderness in her eyes when she'd kissed him. And the fun they'd had staring through the telescope for over an hour before a biting wind had driven them inside. But the most precious moment was when she had fallen asleep on his chest.

"I think…I *know* I am falling in love with her."

Worsley's sigh held grievous disappointment. "One of

the most pervasive vices I've seen. Did you know Lord Jenkins recently fought a most secret duel and almost got himself killed over this damn love argument?"

"I do not want to hear how love is worse than gambling and drinking," Wentworth growled. "I want to know how I can be with her, always."

"So, make an offer—"

"She is not interested in marrying me," he admitted gruffly.

"Now I am interested in meeting her."

His friend was so used to ladies of society attempting to contrive to marry either of them for their wealth, of course Juliana's resistance would be refreshing to his jaded senses.

Wentworth pushed to his feet and went to the high windows overlooking the gas-lit streets of London below. Looking down on the scene from three stories above. Several carriages crawled by, some joining the receiving queue to enter the club.

"I've never seen you in knots over a lady before. If she means that much to you, marry her and keep her by your side."

"You are surprisingly supportive."

The viscount lifted his glass to his lips. "Let's just say I have recent reasons to understand the urges that can plague the heart and torment dreams."

Wentworth jolted. "Good God, you have your own valet."

"More like a governess."

"What need do you have for a governess?"

"It is a long story, my friend. But should you attend the

Duchess of Wycliffe's ball tomorrow, you will see me dance with her."

"You do not dance at society balls."

"For her, I will."

Wentworth smiled, enjoying the notion of his friend being just as knotted in love. "I hope she gives you a merry chase."

Worsley grunted.

And Wentworth thought of all the reasons he and Juliana did not fit. "She is not an English lady. She…she does not fit into the pattern of my life. She is not the kind of person to care about titles."

"So, she does not want to be a countess."

"Or a married woman. But the freedom to be a businesswoman far away from me in bloody New York."

Worsley clapped him on his shoulder.

"If you want her, truly want her, simply learn how you fit into her life."

Then his friend sauntered away, leaving Wentworth alone with his heavy thoughts.

❦

OVER A WEEK HAD FLOWN by since her night in his lordship's bath and bed, and for that duration Juliana had not seen Wentworth. He'd taken himself off to London, and she missed him dreadfully. The ball loomed in three days' time, and she suspected it was that chaos he had escaped. Dozens of servants had been hired from the village to assist for the night. Dozens of flowers were being cut from the nurseries with glass houses that supplied

London's wealthy elite. So late in the year, they were expensive to deliver in pristine condition to his Wiltshire seat. His gamekeepers had been hunting to provide game for the table, and they had ordered other delicacies to cater for the assembled guests. The house bustled with activity, and all the servants were harried to ensure that everything would be perfect for the ball. Only Juliana had been relatively idle.

Juliana escaped it all by staying in Wentworth's room or spending her day near the lake, reading, or chatting with little Tommy. He had been following her around with a suspicious scowl on his little face, until he had confronted her, accusing her of being a girl.

She had not denied it, nor confirmed it, and he hadn't stopped following her about. It had now become their ritual to meet by the lake for luncheon, where she would share whatever prized food she had managed to put together from the kitchens—the perks of being the earl's personal servant. Even so, the cook had made it clear that she was not to get underfoot.

While it felt lonely at times to have no one to chat with beside Tommy, Juliana thought it best to keep a careful distance from the rest of the staff. She was polite and always offered a lending hand when a maid or even a footman needed it. Some of the lads had tried to invite her into the fold by inviting her to play cricket on their off days or to go for a pint in the village.

She always refused with a smile and her head down. It was best to not socialize with the rest of the servants because she did not fit in, and the constant co-mingling would surely reveal her ruse.

The young maid who'd flirted with her so shamelessly had been fired for having a follower from another estate, and Juliana heard whispers that the girl might have been pregnant. But it had ended well because she got engaged, Juliana presumed to the putative father, and they would marry as soon as the banns had been called. Juliana would idly listen to their chattering, for the servants at Norbrook Park had the most up-to-date gossip, but when called upon to take part and offer whatever she heard, Julianna would excuse herself.

"Cor, this is very good," Tommy said, biting into the succulent roast beef she'd rustled up.

He deftly caught the apple she tossed him, and they shared a grin.

"So why ye pretending to be a gent?"

He was persistent.

"Someone is trying to marry me off and I do not want to marry."

His large blue eyes rounded, and his mouth fell opened. "So ye be a lady! I knew the master would not be shucking up to no gent."

She grinned. "But you cannot tell anyone, ever."

He winked conspiratorially and resumed eating.

The crunch of leaves behind Juliana had her whirling around. "You're back!"

At her breathless cry, Tommy looked around. He scrambled to his feet before doffing his hat and dipping into a bow. Wentworth flicked him another coin and his face lit up. Grabbing up the small hamper together with the book, he gave her a careless wave and ran off.

Without overthinking the matter, Juliana rushed into Wentworth's arms and hugged him.

"Ah, so you missed me," he murmured, enfolding his arms around her.

"I did, as much as I trust you missed me."

He grunted, and she laughed, stepping out of the comforting cage of his embrace.

A smile lurked at the corners of his mouth. "How can you tell?"

"You still have on your traveling coat and top hat. You saw me and came over before even going inside."

He framed her face with his gloved hands, and she shivered at the cold feel of them against her skin. But all too soon she grew frightfully warm. Wentworth's lips were barely a whisper over hers. The kiss, so gentle, broke something inside Juliana, and she fisted his jacket and mashed her mouth to his. She swallowed his start of surprise and tempted him to kiss her with all the longing he felt in his heart.

And he did, and soon she was the one seduced, and laden heat surged through her veins. Reluctantly, they parted.

"You stole into my dream every night, since I left Norbrook Park."

"That is only fair since I've been similarly afflicted."

Sudden humor gleamed in his eyes. "Let's return to the main house. I've brought you a present."

Everything felt right now that he was home. *Home*. Her breath hitched. *How do I leave you and return to New York, but how do I stay and give up everything I've wanted for so long?*

❦

THE BALLROOM WAS BRILLIANTLY LIT and humming with music, laughter, and conversation. His aunt and mother had done a stunning job in the weeks they had taken over the running of the manor. Its normal tranquility had been turned upside down, as their orders rang from the rafters and the regular staff and their extra help from the village had run to do the formidable ladies' bidding. Dozens of footmen patrolled with champagne on silver salvers, a twenty-piece orchestra played for the dancing, and outside dozens of lanterns lit paths leading to the gardens and the wide-open lawn.

And at the top of the stairs, the most ravishing creature he'd ever beheld. No one else seemed to notice that a lady arrayed in a dark green gown which clung mouth-watering to her petite frame looked around the ballroom hesitantly. The gown was edged with tiny seed pearls, a charmingly lowered décolletage, and had tiny, puffed sleeves. The golden mask covered her nose, eyes, some of her forehead and her cheek. He'd purchased her a new wig, dark red and caught up in intricate curls. The throng was all too caught up with their own pleasurable pursuits to be aware of the newcomer.

On the journey home, Wentworth had resolved to ask Juliana to be his wife. Not tonight, but before the remaining weeks were up. He would woo her most ardently, and when he was most certain of her love, Wentworth would show her they could fit in each other's lives perfectly.

JULIANA TOOK a deep breath and made her way down the long staircase. Her eyes scanned the people thronging the ballroom of the manor house, searching for only one tall gentleman. There seemed to be so many steps and she hesitated, nervous that Wentworth would be disappointed in her appearance.

With a little laugh, she dismissed that worry. Earlier, staring at herself in the cheval mirror, Juliana owned she had never looked so lovely.

The maid who'd assisted smile and said, "You look beautiful, my lady."

Juliana wondered what the young maid had thought when Wentworth directed her to this room, having instructed her to assist Juliana in getting ready. Perhaps the maid hadn't been suspicious since there were at least a dozen guests staying in his home, but did the maid wonder why she alone had been placed in the family wing?

Juliana glanced down to the foot of the stairs and she saw him waiting. The earl was not wearing a mask. She supposed that it would tangle with his spectacles and that thought amused and strengthened her courage. The rapt look of adoration upon his face bolstered her spirits, and she moved a little quicker, knowing that everything would be perfect when she reached his side.

"I was fearing you would cry off and you promised me a waltz, my Lady Evergreen," he declared.

The music was just coming to an end and he signaled to the orchestra leader silently. At once the beautiful strains of a waltz flowed out through the ballroom.

"Very masterful, my lord," was all Juliana could think to say as he offered her his arm.

"I would be honored if you would allow me the pleasure of this dance, my lady," he said, bowing before leading her out onto the floor.

"Who are all these people? There are so many, I think it must be considered a very popular event, my lord."

"I left everything up to my mother and aunt, do you really want to know them all?" He teased as they glided together as if they were regular dance partners.

"No, the only person I wanted to see was you, Wentworth, but it would be more romantic if it was not such a crush," she said as they avoided an enthusiastic couple who came barreling down the floor and they only turned in time to avoid them.

"And my mother is well pleased with the turnout."

Juliana grinned. "It wouldn't be a success unless ladies and gentlemen were stepping on each other toe."

He tugged her closer to him, twirling her with masculine grace. Pleasure burst in her veins, but as they narrowly avoided another couple Juliana did not think they would dance the night away. The earl was an excellent and most considerate dancer to ensure that they got out of the way of so many collisions.

By the time they finished, they were more breathless from avoiding slamming into other couples, and Juliana was laughing. "I am astonished why that was so much fun."

"Perhaps we should dance in my chambers later in the evening, my lady," he said, smiling down at her, and his eyes promised more than just dancing.

"That would be nice," Juliana said, a dart of hunger crawling through her for this man.

His breath hitched audibly. "I think some of my mother's guests have already over-imbibed and that for your safety we should retreat from the ballroom."

He led her carefully to the edge of the dance floor, struggling through the crowd packing the room.

"Thank you for the dance, Wentworth, even if short, but it is too hot in here for me. I think I will head to the terrace to cool off a little," she said, smiling and hoping he would follow to steal a kiss or two.

"I will fetch some champagne and then join you," he replied, smiling, as she headed for the terrace doors.

It was cooler on the terrace and the sound of the music and crowd was muffled as she moved further away from the ballroom. The colored lanterns made a pretty tableau through the grounds, allowing just enough light to be both mysterious and seductive. Juliana leaned on the balustrade, looking out over the gardens and enjoying her own happiness. Juliana anticipated Wentworth's arrival with excitement and exhilaration. Soon she would be back in his arms and they could slip away from the festivity of the ball and spend some precious moments alone together. She felt a shadow fall over her and a hand brushed her arm. But that was not Wentworth, Juliana was sure, and a shiver of fear ran up her spine. She turned to see Matthew, her stepbrother, smiling at her.

"Juliana, come inside with me at once," he said, pulling her back toward the house. "There is much misunderstanding, and we need to speak right away."

Matthew dragged her toward a door that opened into a

corridor, leading to the library and some of the other rooms that were not in use for the ball. The corridor was but poorly lit and Matthew was stronger than her. She did not want to scream because people would come running and it would create a storm of gossip. His grip seemed to relax a little, and he turned to speak to her, but before he could utter a word, Juliana kicked him hard in the shin and took off as fast as she could.

She pelted down the corridor and made her escape. If she turned down the next corridor, Juliana could make it to the servants' stairs and be out of Matthew's reach. However, she would be safer in the earl's chambers, even Matthew would not dare search there for her.

Just as Juliana was convinced she had shaken off Matthew's pursuit, there was an obstacle in her path. She slammed into the firm but slight chest of a man in evening dress. She glanced up at the man's face and was about to apologize for hitting him, when she realized it was her brother.

A burst of happiness darted through her heart. "Robert, it's wonderful to see you! What are you doing here?" She hugged him tightly to her in relief. "I got your letter, but I thought it would have taken much longer for you to reach England!"

He returned her hug, and then set her from him. "I arrived last week and was most alarmed to hear you had left the viscount's house telling no one. I traveled down with Matthew, our stepbrother, he was very worried about you disappearing…"

"He was the reason I left town. He and the viscount are trying to force me into marriage."

"What?" Robert snapped, his light blue eyes darkening with anger. "He conveniently omitted that part. We were heading to Bath next to see if you were with Mother. A friend of ours, Lord Elgin invited us to come along with him, to this country ball which I see is rather well attended. Come, we shall depart this place and you will tell me why you are here. I have suitable lodgings close by. I've already made arrangements for us to return to New York. We can discuss everything at my lodgings."

Depart this place.

"I am a guest here," she murmured.

"You are?"

"Yes." Juliana swallowed. "Return for me in the morning if you do not stay for the night. You know these events go well beyond the breaking dawn. Is…is our stepfather here as well?"

"I do not know."

"I am heading to my rooms. If they see me, I fear they might still try to take me."

A fierce scowl crossed his handsome face. "I would thrash them within an inch of their lives should they dare. Go, stay inside your room, I will find Matthew and have his explanation for his outrageous conduct."

She kissed his cheek and rushed around him and up the back stairs. If Matthew was there, would her stepfather have come too? Juliana took a steady breath but kept to her original plan and making sure that no one was following or watching her as she headed to the earl's chambers. On her way, she toed off one dancing shoe and then the other, leaving one in the long hallway and one on the stairs.

Wentworth might climb the stairs to find her, and she

had left her slippers as a crumb for him to see where she had gone. Settling in the large armchair near the fire, she tried to ignore the heavy press of dread that had stayed in her heart at her brother's words. How would she say goodbye? It was far too soon. Juliana had expected to have a few more weeks with him.

Oh, Wentworth, please hurry and come to me.

CHAPTER 13

Wentworth couldn't find Juliana. He had made two rounds of the ballroom now, and he did not see her petite, lush form. All the common rooms were empty. He went outside into the gardens, searching to no avail. Almost an hour later, he cursed.

He hurried down the hallway and stopped when he spotted the dancing shoe he'd bought her on the carpeted floor. Stooping, he picked it up. Cinderella, he thought with a dark spurt of amusement. Then he broke into a run, taking the stairs two at a time. He shoved his chamber door open and rushed inside. His bed was empty. His rooms were empty.

A sharp pain shot through him, right into the middle of his chest. Juliana was gone. *Bloody hell.* A soft little sound had him whirling around. She was by the windows, snuggled into a large armchair that almost swallowed her frame.

He blinked, not sure he hadn't somehow conjured her up. But no, she was there, sleeping. The tension that had banded around his chest eased. Wentworth feared she had stolen away from his home, disappearing from his life in the same manner she had entered it, inconspicuously.

As if deep in her sleep she sensed his regard, her lashes fluttered open.

Every emotion he'd felt earlier—the raw, fierce, profound feeling of loss—crashed against his senses. With a gasp, she jerked to her feet, and they met halfway into the room. He took her mouth in a hungry kiss. She returned his embrace, measure for measure, with a passion that startled him. But only for a moment. He framed her face with his hands and ravished her lips thoroughly. Wentworth did not like the desperate ache pummeling his body, but there was nothing he could do to stop it.

She moaned sweet little sounds of pleasure. "I am ready," she pulled away to gasp hotly against his mouth. "With just a kiss I am so wet for you, Wentworth."

A curse came from him, low and fervent. He felt strangely light-headed. He almost resented the feeling of helpless wonder and awe he felt tasting her, touching her. Wentworth yearned to make her his. As he stilled and breathed deeply, he kissed her forehead. He wanted her in his arms every day of his life. And to share kisses and more only with her.

Stepping back, he started to remove his clothes. Juliana smiled. They reached for each other, tugging and removing cravat, shirt, jacket, gown, shift, drawers, and stockings, until they were both utterly naked.

Wentworth had never seen a more perfectly formed lady.

"You are so beautiful," he said, devouring her body.

She stared at him for a long, unblinking moment, then she smiled.

Her breasts were small, but high and firm, with large, berried nipples that had his mouth damn well watering. Her belly was flat and flared into well-rounded hips and a lush backside. Her thighs were slender, white and smooth.

The need to possess her had a sharper edge. The control he'd placed on his passions for so long fractured, and he tugged her to him, flushing her body tight against his. Wentworth swept her into his arms and tossed her onto the center of his bed.

She laughed, the sound a temptation in itself. Then she opened her legs, an invitation he would never resist again.

God, I love you.

THE HUNGRY, driving heat of Wentworth's mouth was on hers. Their kiss grew more feverish and Juliana was agonizingly aware of how hot, hard and huge his manhood was against her swollen sex. Helplessly, her hands rose to his shoulders, clinging to him for support, while his mouth bruised hers with exquisite thoroughness.

He reached between their bodies, and his palm molded to the full mounds of her breasts, his thumbs and forefingers capturing her peaked nipples and rolling them between his fingers. Wentworth's fingers caressed over her quivering belly and down to her sex. He parted her folds delicately, so at odds with the fierce way he took her mouth.

She jerked when those fingers slid through her

growing wetness, up and down, circling around that bundle of nerves. Pleasure quaked through her as the heat low in her belly twisted, became a tight knot of exquisite delight.

The striking pressure against her clitoris increased when he started rubbing her there with two fingers. Up and down, then a press forward. Her legs fell open wider, cradling the power of his body atop hers.

His caress got even firmer, rougher, and an agony of longing swept through Juliana. "Now, Wentworth!" She wasn't altogether certain for what she pleaded, only knowing she needed him to fill the empty ache lingering in her heart and body.

The hot, swollen tip of his manhood pressed against her sensitive entrance. Then he pressed in. She pulled her lips from his, clutching his shoulders and panting at the tight stretch.

They drew a shaky breath together.

He plunged deep, driving past the natural resistance of her body. Her lips parted, but nothing came from her mouth. She couldn't breathe. The pain buffeted her senses in waves.

Juliana shifted and groaned her distress.

"Do not move, Juliana. Though I made sure you would soak my cock, you have a very tight quim. I promise you it will soon ease."

"Kiss me," she said. That would distract her from the burning ache. She always loved his kisses.

And he did until she was moaning and lifting her hips for more. He moved, a slow glide out of her wet, aching sex, and then a deep returning thrust. Juliana screamed.

The pleasure-pain was a burning sensation that started where they connected and spread to her throbbing nub.

Dark, wanton heat spread through her. "Wentworth," she gasped, kissing his shoulders. "I...you make me feel so much."

Another deep stroke, then another and another.

Her wild cries and murmurs dissolved into incoherent fragments.

"Juliana...don't leave...curse it...I..."

She caught the rest of his words with her mouth and poured all the raw emotions pounding through her into the kiss. He leaned forward and pressed his cock deeper inside her sex. He withdrew and thrust, jolting her body under his passionate entry.

Everything inside Juliana centered on the hard, driving thrusts of his cock into her wet channel. He swallowed her whimpers and moans, stroking in and out of her, all control abandoned. Hot darts of pleasure shook her, unlike anything Juliana felt before.

"Wentworth," she gasped, almost frightened at the intensity of the sensations blossoming through her entire body.

A heavy ache coiled low in her stomach, drawing tighter as the sensations intensified until Juliana convulsed beneath him, twisting, crying out. With a few jerky thrusts, and a harsh groan, he emptied deep inside her shivering body. They stayed like that for a long time until her lashes fluttered closed. She barely felt when he withdrew from her body, cleaned her, and drew the sheets to her shoulders. Juliana fell asleep with a smile on her mouth but an ache in her heart.

How do I ever leave this…us?

A FEW HOURS LATER, Juliana sat near the edge of the bed, her legs folded beneath her as she watched the rise and fall on Wentworth's chest. Last night he'd been about to ask her to stay and she had kissed the words away, filled with fright, uncertainty and soul burning love. He had taken her to the heights of bliss several times, and she was smart enough to know there might be consequences to their fiery passion. There might be a child, one who she would nurture with all the love in her heart, and one who would inherit the empire she would build with Robert.

Slipping from the bed, she winced at the ache in her muscles and the soreness between her thighs. They might have been too enthusiastic. She padded over to the table, opened the drawer, and withdrew a sheaf of paper along with the quill, inkwell, and ink blotter.

Dearest Wentworth,

It is exceedingly difficult for me to bid you farewell. You see, I am falling in love with you, and I am certain I am more than halfway there. Since living in England, these last few weeks with you have been my happiest.

The whimsical part of me wants to believe I can abandon all the dreams I've had for the last several years and stay with you here in England. We could marry, theoretically, and I could try to fit into the position of the countess to a particular English earl. I could try harder to be properly correct and I might succeed, even though there are times I fear I would risk causing a scandal. I could also dearly hope your mother would accept 'one of those brash American girls with no decorum' she spoke about during dinner. We might even be happy for a while, but it would eventually fade because the dreams I have are very important to me.

I do hope you understand, and I dearly wish we might remain friends and correspond with each other from across the oceans. Perhaps you might even visit me one day in New York, and I hope even more ardently should I visit England again you'll receive me cordially.

Forgive me for not being able to part with you directly.

Yours,

Juliana.

She hurried into the bath chamber and tidied herself as best as she could without turning on the spigot. Then she dressed in her valet clothes for the day and secured her wig. But Juliana did not lay out his clothes or polish his boots. She slipped out of the room, startled to note it was almost noon.

Good heavens. Could any of the maids have slipped inside, seen them curled into the bed and went away? She spied her brother speaking with the younger twin. She cleared her throat, and Robert at a glance dismissed her. Then he did a very comical double take. She lifted her chin to a door down the hallway, then made her way there and inside the small rose parlor. A few seconds later, he entered.

"Juliana?"

"Yes, it's me."

"Why in God's name are you dressed so?"

"It is a long story, and I will tell you on the way. We must leave immediately."

"I will have the story now," he said with a thunderous expression.

She rolled her eyes and quickly relayed it.

"A valet," he said faintly. "As in servant to the earl, often alone with the earl in his private chambers?"

"I cannot credit that part is what have you angry. Not that the viscount and that dreadful buffoon you called a friend tried to kidnap me and force me into a marriage?"

Robert sighed. "I meant to tell you it all, last night I spoke with Matthew, he doesn't want to marry you either. It's the viscount's dictate, and he was damn glad when you disappeared. He is in love with a governess working in the Fenton's household, but our stepfather won't hear of the match."

"Rubbish! He was there that night in the carriage when I came to, trussed up."

"Yes, and if you had allowed him an explanation before you knocked him over the head, you would have heard the tale that he is already married in secret and cannot do his father's will."

"Married?"

"Yes."

Juliana almost laughed. All her grand adventures had been for naught. She hadn't needed to be here at Norbrook Park for the last few weeks!

But I would have missed ever meeting Wentworth, had I not been here.

And truly, she could find no regret inside, only a heavy feeling of sadness and a deep rush of want. "We must leave now. We will discuss everything else in the carriage."

She'd already wasted at least five minutes with this conversation.

"We must wait until the earl—"

"No!" Juliana closed her eyes to stop the prick of tears. "I cannot see him! We must leave before he wakes."

Her brother frowned, widening his pale-blue eyes. "Juliana, we cannot abuse his hospitality—"

"If I see him, I'll not be able to leave," she confessed.

Robert laughed, a soft sound of disbelief. "You mean stay here…with the earl?"

"Yes."

Anger flashed in his eyes. "Have you lost your senses? How could you so easily forget the dreams of our father and the plans we made? For what?"

He stared at her as if he did not know her.

"That is why I said we should go now."

Without saying another word, her brother whirled around, anger and disappointment evident in every line of his lanky body. She followed behind him at a discreet pace, aware she still played the role of a servant.

He bid the countess farewell and left his regards for the earl before asking for their carriage to be brought around.

Walking away from Wentworth and the place she had been happiest, felt like walking barefoot on knives. She entered the carriage first, folding her hand across her chest. Her belly felt knotted, like the beginning of a stomachache that might last for painful hours. The carriage rattled along, and she thought she heard a shout over the crunch of the gravel-lined driveway. Against her better judgment, she took a quick glance over her shoulder and choked on the air.

"Stop the carriage!"

"GOOD HEAVENS, Wentworth, whatever are you about?" the countess cried when he ran past her in the hallway dressed only in his trousers.

Two housemaids gasped before dissolving into giggles, and his Aunt Millicent seemed ready to swoon. The butler remained stoic and even opened the door for his master.

Wentworth reached the steps of his manor just as the carriage rumbled down the long driveway.

"Juliana!" he shouted, uncaring that he made a spectacle of himself in front of his family and staff.

His heart pounded a vicious beat, and his damn throat ached. Why had he wasted time reading the letter and putting on trousers? The carriage stopped, and he saw the curtains by the small window parted and Juliana's face peeked out.

"Isn't that your valet?" his cousin asked.

"His valet," his mother gasped. "The person you chase after in this awful and scandalous state of déshabille is your valet?"

"If I had not been here to witness it, I for one would not have believed a word of it," Aunt Millicent said in shocked tones. "You *are* aware you are without clothes, Wentworth?"

"Millie, I cannot understand it," his mother said fretfully. "He is chasing after the coach that left with his manservant. I...I...could it be this is why he has shown no lady any regard over the years?"

Aunt Millicent gasped and he could feel their stares, but the only thing that concerned Wentworth was the stopped carriage. Realizing she truly meant to leave him, and with no sort of farewell, left him feeling crushed and almost breathless. His chest lifted on a ragged exhalation and his fingers tightened over the damn letter she'd left behind.

That was it, a letter with words showing her fear and her longing. At first, he'd felt a visceral dread that he'd scared Juliana with the intensity of his ardor. But he'd re-read her words, and in a nutshell, loving him meant letting go of her dreams.

The woman he'd fallen in love with had no faith in him. Did she believe the love he offered was one so selfish he would only care about his desires?

Have I ever shown her anything else?

He dearly hoped he had, but Wentworth admitted he had been too caught up with falling for her, that he hadn't explained or told her he wanted to be by her side forever. Nor had he told her that he would love her eternally or for however long, God would give them as man and wife. And he would damn well find her in the next lifetime.

ROBERT FISHED out his pocket watch for the third time, a black scowl forming on his face.

"We must go now, Juliana."

"I need a few more minutes," she said, her throat

burning.

"I see the turmoil in your eyes, and I do not understand it," he murmured. "You spent almost four weeks here at Norbrook Park, and you are conflicted over the earl. Has he offered you words of love?"

The sudden ache in her throat prevented her from replying right away. Finally, she said, "Yes."

Her brother froze. "And do you love him too?"

She noted that one of his gloved hands was gripping the edge of the carriage seat as if it were a lifeline. Her response mattered very much to her brother, and she understood. He was only two years older than her, and they had always been close. At the death of papa, when mama had shut them out in her wild and unstoppable grief, they had anchored each other.

He had been her best friend for so long. The future they dreamed about, they had planned it together. Always.

"Did you not expect me to fall in love one day?" she asked hoarsely.

"Jules," he began gruffly. "You hate it here in England. We only stayed this long for mother and she is now happy with that bounder she married. He even genuinely dotes on her. There is nothing keeping us here, nothing keeping you here. This…whatever happened with you and him. This was just a fleeting moment. In New York there is everything. Our old friends keen for your return. Our business interests. Papa's dreams of building a legacy for our future children."

Her lips trembled with her smile. "I suppose we can only have those children with people from New York."

"Home, Julie. Home."

And then he rapped the roof of the carriage, and it lurched into motion.

❦

WENTWORTH FELT as if someone had ripped his whole heart from his chest. The carriage drove away, gradually picking up speed as the coachman urged the team of four onward. He had all but run down the steps, ignoring the gravel stones that dug into the soles of his feet. Fucking hell. He stopped when the carriage disappeared round the bend and into a row of large beech trees.

"Order my fastest horse to be readied," he said to the stable lad who hovered, staring with wide eyes.

In truth, several of his servants had audaciously come outside and gawked.

His mother's pale face had gone paler and her eyes were wide with worry or perhaps shock.

"Wentworth," she said sharply. "It is cold out and you are without proper garments. Your chest is bared and your feet! You'll catch your death."

Yet he could not move, trying to sort out the jumbled voices in his thoughts. The first time he'd seen her, the smile, the way she'd spoken low and husky to maintain her disguise, the way they had hunted together, the cottage, star gazing, making love.

"How could…" his throat closed. "So easily?"

His mother touched his arm, and he glanced down into her concerned eyes. "You are wondering how your valet could leave so easily?"

He nodded, unable to give voice to the emotions

tearing through him.

"Perhaps," his mother began gently, "Perhaps he did it because…because such a relationship will be frowned upon and be extremely hard to…hide from society."

What?

"My valet is a lady."

His mother's lips parted, and she pinched him.

"Such scandalous behavior!"

Aunt Millicent hurried over. "What is it?"

"The valet is a lady!" his mother hissed in a furious undertone.

"A *lady*?" Aunt Millicent sent him a look of deep admiration. "I never knew you had it in you. I am so proud."

"You love her," his mother said. "I cannot credit any of this is happening and in front of the servants! This will be all over the country by this evening."

Wentworth hardly gave a damn. A hole had opened inside and he wondered if the hollowness would ever abate.

She had left. The brave, witty and kind woman he'd fallen in love with had left without a backward glance.

"What will you do?" Aunt Millicent demanded briskly.

"Why, he will forget that little miscreant. If she had any feelings for my son, she would have—"

"Chase her," he said gruffly. "I am going after her… and it might take me as far as New York."

"Parliament is far more important."

"Mother, please, I love her. And I'll not marry anyone, if I cannot have Juliana. She makes…she makes me feel and hunger to live in a world outside my books, and when

I do get lost in them she is there, a shadow in my mind, teasing me and still reminding me that someone is there waiting for me to close those pages. I…I cannot begin to explain what she means to me. Another person's reason or logic will not compel me when it comes to her. Understand this."

His mother stared at him like a creature who had popped into the courtyard, and her eyes watered.

"Then go for her, but I shall never like this lady for hurting your heart so!"

"I…" His words faltered and his heart jolted as he spied a slim figure in the distance hurrying up the long driveway. *Was it…?* Wentworth walked forward, wincing slightly at the sharp stab into his sole.

"I think the valet is returning," Henrietta called from where she stood with her sister, the butler, and perhaps all thirty-five staff of the estate.

"D'ya think its dem books wot finally did it?" he heard a gardener mutter.

Wentworth walked to meet her, moving slowly because of the damnable stones. She looked behind her and he spied her brother running after her. She ran toward Wentworth and as she grew closer, he stopped.

"Why is she running, do you think?" Aunt Millicent demanded.

A quick glance over his shoulder showed his mother, aunt, and several of his outdoor servants following him! Wentworth ignored them and turned to Juliana, who had stopped some feet away, her wide eyes staring beyond his shoulders.

"You came back," he said gruffly. "Why?"

She shook her head wordlessly and pressed three trembling fingers over her mouth.

"Why is the bleeding valet crying?" a perplexed voice asked, and his mother made a hushing sound.

Wentworth bit back the roar rising in his throat and took another step toward her.

Her panting brother reached, his expression thunderous.

"You jumped from a moving carriage!" he snapped. "Have you gone mad?"

"You would not stop," she said, but she never took her eyes from Wentworth. "I asked you to stop."

"Why?" he demanded, baffled. "Why did I need to stop?"

"Because I could not leave without seeing…without seeing you," she whispered. "I should never have left just a letter. It was cowardly, and my papa did not raise a coward."

"So, you mean to tell me then that you are leaving?" Wentworth asked, his words chilled, for an anger was storming through his heart. He wanted to slam his fist into a wall. Perhaps the physical pain would diminish the one in his heart. She'd only returned to prove she wasn't a coward. "Then go!"

But she did not move.

"I cannot leave, Wentworth," she said, and in her eyes he spied a longing that almost felled him to his knees.

"Why not?" he demanded gruffly.

Her gaze skipped to behind him once more, and a delicate flush covered her face.

"You know," she whispered.

"I do not know," he said, flatly.

"My letter—"

"Juliana," he said firmly, "I do not know."

"Juliana—" her brother began.

"Shut the fucking hell up," Wentworth snapped, "Or by God, I'll not be responsible for my actions."

Her brother firmed his lips and his eyes narrowed, but his mouth thankfully remained closed.

"The dreams you speak of, Robert, of building our legacy and returning to our friends and family in New York I mean to fulfill. As you said earlier, the weeks here with the earl are nothing compared to fulfilling the wishes of our father. However, I must tell you that the connection I feel with Wentworth is far more profound. And I am ever so grateful I ran to him, for I have found something I...I never want to exist without."

All the apprehension drained away, replaced by delight. The hollowness retreated and his heart surged back to life, pounding wildly.

"I love you," she said. Juliana's voice was not steady but quavered with her feelings. "Thoughts and dreams of more money or businesses have never given me the happiness I feel with you. With you I dream of...of bathtubs...and star gazing, laughing, and walking in the woods, discussing ventures, even gossiping about the locals. With you I see a future rich in laughter and children and anything I want because I finally understand what I have been seeing in your eyes. It is love...one that will lift me up unconditionally."

No one spoke.

"I would have chased you to the end of the world...

and then I would have stayed by your side," he said gruffly, holding out his arms.

With a sob, she hurtled toward him and flung herself into his embrace, raining kisses over her chin and jaw.

"Utterly scandalous *and* so delightful!" Henrietta cried somewhere behind them.

Wentworth ignored whoever still lingered, hugging Juliana tightly in his arms. "I love you," he said against her temple. "I love you so damn much, Juliana. Marry me."

"Yes." She lifted her face from where it had been buried against his throat. She touched a gentle finger to the corner of his mouth. "Yes. For our honeymoon, I want to show you New York."

He brushed the lightest kiss against her mouth. "I vow to you I shall never disappoint you. Nor fail to do everything within my power to see your dreams fulfilled."

Then he turned around to see the staff had dispersed, his mother and aunt taking them to task and shooing them away in the distance.

"I'll line them up and give them a most severe lecture," he said. "Should they dare relate any scandal from our home, we'll sack them."

She laughed. "Now would also be a good time to inform them of their generous end-of-year bonus."

"An excellent move that."

"I know," she said smugly. Then she sobered, shifting around to see her brother walking away.

"Robert!"

He paused.

"I am not giving up! I intend to follow the dreams I had."

He made no reply, but he remained still.

"I am simply expanding them into something far richer and beautiful. I promise we will visit New York often and we shall write each other all the time."

He turned around, and it humbled Wentworth to see that the man's eyes were dampened. He walked toward him, and Robert met him halfway.

Wentworth held out his hand, and her brother took it.

"I'll cherish and protect her for all of our days. Your blessing would make Juliana happy."

Robert's gaze swept over him, taking in Wentworth's bare chest and feet.

"Are you certain you are an earl?"

"I was always different."

The man smiled. "I do believe you suit each other well. Juliana was always a little different too."

He stepped back, held out his arms, and she walked into them, hugging her brother. "I love you, Robert."

He smiled. "I love you too. I will remain in England for a short time. No need to rush home now that you're staying."

She pulled away, laughing delighted. "How long will you stay for?"

"Until the wedding."

"Why, that is at least a year—"

"We'll be married by next week, with our honeymoon to New York in short succession," Wentworth said. How could she imagine he would allow her to wait so long to become his wife, his lover, his countess?

She rushed back into his arms, laughing as she kissed his mouth. Forgetting about her brother as if the man did not stand there watching them, she kissed Wentworth with breathtaking sweetness.

Four weeks later…

"I CANNOT BELIEVE Christmas is next week," Juliana said, fitting a pine cone into the large Christmas tree decorating the large drawing room.

"I still cannot believe you are my wife."

She sent him a scandalized look. "That is what you cannot believe? Even though we celebrate that happy event so wickedly repeatedly every night and then sneak away often during the days."

A choking sound came from the doorway, and they both looked around to see his mother standing there, her cheeks red.

"Oh!" Juliana said, and then it was her turn to blush.

Wentworth chuckled unashamedly and winked at his countess. She tried to pinch his arm discreetly but his mother saw, for an amused gleam entered her gaze.

"I purchased a few gifts for the servants and wondered where to leave them," the dowager countess stated, trying to correctly pretend not hearing Juliana's words.

Juliana's eyes lit up. "I went into the village and bought them all gifts."

Juliana and his mother left the room, their head bent close. As he stared after them, a powerful feeling of happiness swelled through Wentworth's heart. He was damn glad his wife had such a lush backside. If he hadn't been so distracted perhaps he would have been so ensconced in his scholarly pursuits he would have missed her.

Immediately he dismissed the notion.

If not her lush derriere, her eyes, or her smile, *something* would have arrested his attention upon her, and that experiment would have still happened.

He concluded the experiment had been a total success with perfect results. So great he might even write a paper about it, tentatively titled, *A Rogue in the Making*. It was an experiment that he was happy to spend the rest of his life continuing and enjoying.

❦

THANK you for reading **A Rogue in the Making**!

I hope you enjoyed the journey to happy ever after for Wentworth & Juliana. **REVIEWS ARE GOLD TO AUTHORS,** for they are a very important part of reaching readers, and I do hope you will consider leaving an honest review on Amazon adding to my rainbow. It does not have to be lengthy, a simple sentence or two will do. Just know that I will appreciate your efforts sincerely.

If you loved that sneak peek at Viscount Worsley, he has his own book—Sins of Viscount Worsley, and if you've not read it, you can grab a copy here!

For more from the Forever Yours Series you can grab a copy of ***My One and Only Earl,*** the next book in the series.

Grab a Copy!

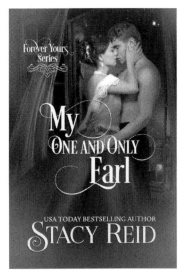

Grab A Copy!

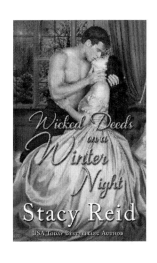

ACKNOWLEDGMENTS

I thank God every day for my family, friends, and my writing. A special thank you to my husband. I love you so hard! Without your encouragement and steadfast support I would not be living my dream of being an author. You encourage me to dream and are always steadfast in your wonderful support. You read all my drafts, offer such amazing insight and encouragement. Thank you for designing my fabulous cover! Thank you for reminding me I am a warrior when I wanted to give up on so many things.

Thank you, Giselle Marks for being so wonderful and supportive always. You are a great critique partner and friend. Readers, thank you for giving me a chance and reading my book! I hope you enjoyed and would consider leaving a review. Thank you!

ABOUT STACY

USA Today Bestselling author Stacy Reid writes sensual Historical and Paranormal Romances and is the published author of over twenty books. Her debut novella The Duke's Shotgun Wedding was a 2015 HOLT Award of Merit recipient in the Romance Novella category, and her bestselling Wedded by Scandal series is recommended as Top picks at Night Owl Reviews, Fresh Fiction Reviews, and The Romance Reviews.

Stacy lives a lot in the worlds she creates and actively speaks to her characters (aloud). She has a warrior way "Never give up on dreams!" When she's not writing, Stacy spends a copious amount of time binge-watching series like The Walking Dead, Altered Carbon, Rise of the Phoenixes, Ten Miles of Peach Blossom, and playing video games with her love. She also has a weakness for ice cream and will have it as her main course.

Stacy is represented by Jill Marshall at Marsal Lyon Literary Agency.

She is always happy to hear from readers and would love to connect with you via my Website, Facebook, and Twitter. To be the first to hear about her new releases, get cover reveals, and excerpts you won't find anywhere else, sign up for her newsletter, or join her over at Historical Hellions, her fan group!

Printed in Great Britain
by Amazon

76189720R00121